3

Bitter Range

Frank Shannon arrived home from the war to find his family dynasty torn apart. Who was Jack Bamber, the lean stranger living in Tom Shannon's Slash S ranch house? And where was Tom and his wife, Beth?

Locked in a cell and accused of cattle rustling, Shannon vows to discover the truth. With the help of veteran lawyer Mack Findlay and an unlikely alliance with Marshal Eli Simm, Shannon begins unravelling a fifty-year-old mystery that is destined to end with the thunder of hooves and the roar of blazing six-guns.

By the same author

Hanging at Horse Creek
Shootout at Casa Grande
Bloody Trail to Dorado
Hannahan's Lode

Bitter Range

JIM LAWLESS

A Black Horse Western

ROBERT HALE · LONDON

© Jim Lawless 2006
First published in Great Britain 2006

ISBN-10: 0-7090-7972-9
ISBN-13: 978-0-7090-7972-9

Robert Hale Limited
Clerkenwell House
Clerkenwell Green
London EC1R 0HT

Typeset by
Derek Doyle & Associates, Shaw Heath.
Printed and bound in Great Britain by
Antony Rowe Limited, Wiltshire.

ONE

It took Frank Shannon three years and a thousand miles of wandering to make it home from the war. When he crossed Crooked Creek and pushed the roan up the steep bank onto hauntingly familiar range that lay between there and Dodge City, the weight of those years fell away from him as if on that sweet, warm Kansas day he had, once and for all, discarded his heavy military topcoat.

His lean, hard body carried a scar from a sabre slash picked up at the first Bull Run, others from bullet and knife wounds inflicted by scar-faced bandits and evil-eyed renegades he had faced and vanquished in bars and cantinas across a wide swathe of Mexico and the West. Outwardly he was erect, clear-eyed, a confident man at ease with himself; a man not to be crossed. Mentally, and for reasons all too clear to him, he knew he was burnt out.

Time had taken its toll but he had crossed the fragile line between whole man and broken has-been outside a Texas bank when, paradoxically, he had finished putting money in rather than withdrawing it with menace. The bank robber that day was a big man with straggly grey hair, a black bandanna covering the lower half of his face and a shotgun brandished wildly. In a hollow well of silence, he had left behind him ashen-faced bank clerks with upstretched hands, and had been making his escape. Clutching a heavy gunny sack, he had collided with Shannon as he backed out of the door and, pale eyes wide with shock, had turned and pulled the trigger.

But Shannon was already down, dropping instinctively as his hand stabbed for his six-gun. The shotgun's hot blast went over his head. Thirty yards away, a woman in a long dress had been blown backwards into the dusty street, her bodice a bloody mess. And, with a sharp pain like a sliver of ice piercing his brain, Frank Shannon had shot the bank robber between the eyes.

He had ridden with those stark memories for the past twelve months: a woman's white face, her blood a dark pool in the dry dust; a grey-haired man on his back in the street with a black bandanna covering his mouth and nose, in his lifeless hand a shotgun with smoking muzzles, his dead eyes glittering in the sun. And he had taken steps to drown them, or what he considered uncompromisingly to be his own weakness, by resorting to the whiskey bottle.

But he knew the homecoming would change all that.

In his saddle-bag, given to him high in the Cimarron Range of New Mexico territory by a bearded trapper stinking of bear grease, he carried one last bottle of moonshine whiskey that was as potent as snake venom. It was almost empty. In the last long miles that saw him come tumbling down from those hills to follow the snaking course of the Beaver river, swing north into Kansas, cross the Cimarron and ride on towards Crooked Creek, he had been over-whelmed by the weight of wasted years. So he had clung to that bottle, put his trust in its ability to dull festering wounds as a man would trust a loyal friend – but the comfort he gained came at its usual loathsome price.

When he splashed down the bank into Crooked Creek he was a drunk clinging to the saddle horn, a man seemingly too dazed by harsh liquor for coherent thought yet managing, some-how, to mumble over and over again the mantra that drove him on: the life that lay ahead would banish forever the troubles of his past.

That promise was the bright beacon that had drawn him across the border at Laredo, and pushed him every mile of the long ride north to Kansas.

But with that journey drawing to its close, with sanctuary but a few short miles away, a sober Frank Shannon would have heeded the hard lessons he had learned during those troubled years and been wiser and certainly less sanguine.

It was late summer, and in the twilight the winds sweeping across the Kansas plains bore a chill that cut through the alcoholic haze and went a little way towards clearing his head. Racking his sluggish brain as the patient roan carried him steadily northward, squinting at flat terrain and a sea of grass that was at once familiar and strange, he calculated that he was already on land owned by his family but still half a day's ride from the ranch.

That settled, he rode until it was full dark and pushed on grimly again for a further ten miles, navigating by the stars. Then, exhausted, head pounding, he turned off open grassland and, in a stand of cottonwoods alongside the sparkle of a moonlit creek, saw to the roan, unrolled his blankets and bedded down for the night.

But before he did that, before contemplating sleep, he drained the bottle of moonshine whiskey and for the last time tasted the fiery liquid that had sustained him for so long.

Then he smashed the bottle on a rock and buried the glittering fragments in a hole he dug with his knife.

His wanderings were over. The past was dead.

He awoke to a pounding head, a mouth as dry as the Staked Plains and in his nostrils the faint smell of wood smoke. And something else. He frowned, rolled, came up out of his blankets and at once dry retched; saw saddle and saddle-bags against the bole of a tree and made an unsteady lunge for his canteen. The water was like warm nectar. He gulped it greedily, out of the corner of his eye caught a glimpse of the fresh earth where the shattered bottle was buried, and managed a wry smile as he wiped his mouth on his sleeve.

The roan was thirty yards away, hobbled, standing hip-shot and patient. Shannon found his hat, emptied the canteen into it and gave the horse a drink. Then he flipped the Stetson towards his rumpled blankets, stretched, and sniffed the air.

Burnt hide. That was what he could smell mingled with the smoke from a camp-fire. Only camp-fire wasn't quite right, because the burnt hide told a story that suggested the fire was more than a heap of glowing embers fit only for brewing coffee.

He walked further away from the cottonwoods fringing the creek, topped a low rise, looked down into a shallow depression. There, below him, was the fire. Red embers smouldering within a crude hearth of blackened rocks. A few yards away, a cow. Dead.

Shannon's breath hissed through his nostrils. Within him, uneasiness stirred like a sickness. He looked about him, followed the cottonwoods with his eyes to where the creek curled around in a tight oxbow – saw nothing moving.

He swallowed drily, thought longingly of the tepid water, then made his way down the slope.

The fire was hot on his face. He looked around at hard earth cut by the sharp hooves of a small herd of cattle; looked closer and found the sign of just the one horse and knew he had slept drunkenly while in the dawn light one man had been at work. He crossed to the dead cow. There was a bloody calf next to it: the birth had killed them both. Shannon dropped to his haunches, reached out to smooth the hide with his fingers. And swore softly.

Slash S. The Shannon brand. Scrawled on a scrap of paper fifty years ago by his grandpa, Jesse Shannon, in the soddy that was his first Kansas home. Branded on the half dozen longhorns that comprised his first herd. And, in the years that followed, recognized by everyone within a thousand square miles as the brand of the Shannon family who had built up a cattle empire and founded the town that bore their name. Shannon Plains. The settlement that had sprung up on their land and was in every sense a part of the ranch, a part of the Shannon dynasty.

By Frank Shannon's reckoning, the town was

just out of sight over the horizon.

And here, in front of him, the clear evidence that someone was rustling Shannon cattle. The Slash S was smudged, the hair around it singed. Crude attempts had been made to burn in another brand, unfinished because the animal had died. His night ruined by the death of the cow, the lone rustler had given it up as a bad job, and hightailed.

Shannon patted the dead cow, let his eyes drift sideways; saw the rustler's running iron lying half in the fire. Angry now, not thinking, he reached out, picked up the iron and at once dropped it on the rocks as the hot metal seared his fingers. Cursing, the ringing of the iron echoing in his ears, he rocked back on his heels, clamped his burnt hand in his armpit as breath hissed through his teeth.

When he looked up, a tall man with cold blue eyes was looking at him along the barrel of a rifle.

TWO

They had come out of the cottonwoods on foot, four of them, cowhands all, but the big man who now approached him under the watchful gaze of the man with the rifle was clearly the one in authority. The Slash S foreman, Frank Shannon figured. That meant the man worked for his pa, Tom Shannon. . . .

'You can put up the rifle,' Shannon said, rising. 'I'm Frank Shannon, Tom Shannon's son.'

'Last I heard,' the man with the rifle said, 'young Frank went away to war – and stayed away.'

'For the war, then three more years,' Shannon said. 'But now I'm back.'

'From where I stand,' the big man said, his voice flat and uninterested, 'you look like a stranger caught making a bungled job of stealing another man's cattle.'

'I don't expect you to take my word for anything,' Shannon said. 'I'll ride to the house

12

with you, willingly. You don't need your weapons.'

He stared deliberately at the rifle, lifted his eyes to meet the blue-eyed man's gaze, saw the wolfish grin as the rifle was lowered and cradled on a forearm.

'I'll decide what we do with our weapons,' the big man said. 'But if we ride to the big house, you won't be carrying yours.'

Shannon shook his head. 'I told you, your boss is my father – and I don't see that as a reason for giving up my guns.'

The big man smiled distantly, lifted a hand to wave away two of the men. They turned to walk back towards the cottonwoods. For the horses, Shannon figured. The man with the sharp blue eyes wandered close to the fire, nudged the running iron with the toe of his boot. But his glance never strayed far from Shannon, his hands remained firmly on the rifle.

'I'm Deek Lancer, Slash S foreman. The man lookin' at your handiwork is Cole Dyson.' The big man was looking critically at Shannon's appearance. His nostrils twitched, and Shannon guessed he'd caught the stink of hard liquor. 'You tell me you're riding home.'

'And now I'm telling you again,' Shannon said. 'Tom Shannon's my pa. It's taken me a long while and a lot of miles to make it, but that's neither here nor there. I rode onto Shannon land last night, bedded down. This morning I woke up, found this. . . .' He waved a hand at the fire, the running iron, the dead cow with its calf.

'You sleep real sound,' Lancer said with obvious disbelief.

'I was drunk.'

'And now you're lying.'

'No.'

As if no longer considering Shannon a threat, or perhaps guided by some unseen signal from his boss, Cole Dyson now left the fire and started towards the trees. He had the hot running iron held gingerly in one hand. Evidence, Shannon thought – as if any were needed; and he knew that with those three men no more than thirty yards away there was little chance of getting away from Lancer, of extricating himself from what was turning into a dangerous situation.

But why should he need to? He was on his pa's land, the only son, heir to the whole damn Shannon shebang.

Lancer was watching him, observing his silence. He seemed amused by Shannon's predicament – or perhaps by something else. Then he heard the two men approaching with the horses. He watched Dyson stop them, wrap the iron in a rag and drop it in a saddle-bag, then mount up. A smile flickered across Lancer's face. He stepped forward, kicked earth and stones over the hot embers, stamped his boots and looked at Shannon.

'All right. Go collect your gear, get back here. And don't get ideas about ridin' off. I'll take you to the house, see what they've got to say.'

There was no more mention of disarming his prisoner. Feeling relief, a sudden relaxation of muscles he hadn't known were tense, Frank Shannon left the four men in the hollow and went back to where he had spent the night. While he packed up he was aware of the blue-eyed rifleman, Cole Dyson, watching him from the ridge. But that didn't matter.

The trees were close enough and high enough for them to have hanged him for rustling Tom Shannon's cattle.

Instead, they were taking him home.

They rode for half an hour, Lancer and Dyson a little way in front of Shannon, the two dour men who had spoken not a word some thirty yards behind him. It was a tactic Shannon appreciated, for he knew that an escort riding any closer would risk being overpowered if he launched a surprise attack, any further back and there would be space and time for him to make a sudden break and get clean away.

Yesterday he had sensed he was on Shannon land without clearly recognizing any feature. Now, as the remaining miles were eaten up by the steady pace of the Slash S riders, the knowledge that he was home which had been a subconscious feeling was being confirmed by sights and sounds he recalled from his childhood: trees in whose bark he had carved his name with bruised fingers holding his first sharp knife; the gurgle of creeks where he had swum naked in the long hot summers; the rocky bluff, on a bend in the trail, where his first pony had dropped a hoof in a gopher hole and broken its leg.

He lifted his head, sniffing the air, his eyes ranging left, right and far ahead. His heartbeat quickened. They crossed prairie where cattle grazed, rode in oppressive silence and mounting tension until, in the distance, the low smudge of white buildings marking the Shannon family's sprawling ranch house, barns and corrals could be seen against the wider clutter of random shapes that was the nearby town – Shannon Plains.

And then they were riding through the gates, underneath the heavy board spanning the trail that bore the legend 'Slash S', on up the curving approach that skirted the corrals, over the hump and down the easy slope past barns and trees that had been old when Jesse Shannon left his soddy and dug the foundations of his first *real* home.

The big foreman drew rein in front of the house. Shannon and the other three riders pulled in behind him as he dismounted, squared his shoulders and walked up the path to the wide gallery and the front door.

He knocked. Pulled off his Stetson and slapped it against his legs. Stepped back a pace.

The front door opened.

From the dark interior a stranger emerged. Tall. Lean. Silver hair over a face deeply lined. Belly flat and hard behind a broad belt with a dull steel buckle.

And from thirty fcct away, Frank Shannon listened in disbelief to Deek Lancer's words.

'We caught this man just after sun up, on Slash S land. A dead cow and calf alongside a fire. He was holding a hot running iron. Says he's Frank Shannon.'

'Now hold on a minute,' Shannon said hotly, and he swung out of the saddle and started up the path as the blue-eyed man leaned over to grab his shoulder. Shannon shook him off. He heard a soft curse as Dyson sprang from his horse and started after him, saw the rawboned man in the doorway lift a hand.

'Leave him be.'

Shannon ran up the steps, crossed the gallery. Lancer replaced his hat to leave both his hands free. He stepped to one side. His right hand drifted towards his holster as he kept one eye on Shannon, the other on the man in the doorway.

'Who the hell are you?'

'My name is Jack Bamber.' Grey eyes as cold as winter snow looked Shannon up and down.

'Where's my pa?'

Bamber shrugged. 'Shannon's not here.'

'You mean he's out? Gone to town?' Shannon felt bewildered.

'I don't know where he is.'

'Then what are you doing in his house?'

Bamber pursed his lips, then shook his head. 'This is my house. And now I'm asking you to explain what you were doing with a running iron and one of my cows.'

'Oh, no,' Shannon said. 'A Slash S cow, all the cattle here are my father's—'

'Your father owns no cattle,' Bamber said, 'if, in fact, you are Shannon's son. He has no land. He has no house worthy of the name; he and his wife live in a shack somewhere in the hills.' He stared dispassionately. 'You say you're Frank Shannon. That may be so, but by the look of you, the stink of you. . . .' He let his meaning sink in as Shannon mentally cursed his dust-stained clothes, his unshaven face, the reek of alcohol that was like dirt ingrained in his skin.

'My gut reaction to what's happened this morning,' Bamber went on, 'is that we've got our hands on the man behind the rustling that's been steadily depleting my herds—'

'Slash S herds!'

'Yes. My herds. I am Slash S.'

'No,' Shannon said. His voice was choked. He had taken a step backwards. Rage and despair were welling inside him like a terrible sickness.

18

'The Shannon dynasty stretches back generations. Shannon Plains was founded by my
grandpa; my father carried on the line.
Something that big, that powerful, can't be wiped
out on the say so of a fool posturing in a house
doesn't belong to him, doesn't—'

Anger was making him babble. Shannon broke
off, shaking his head. But already he had said too
much. The big man in the doorway, his urbanity
gone, his thin face dark with anger, looked
beyond Shannon and gave a curt nod.

And the last Shannon remembered as a mighty
blow drove him to his knees and lightning flared
red, was the look in those wintry grey eyes, a look
that followed him like his worst nightmare into
infinite blackness.

THREE

Deek Lancer and Cole Dyson took him into town, his wrists tied painfully to the horn with rawhide thongs, his body drooping as the horse's jolting gait stabbed at his throbbing head. His gunbelt was draped over Dyson's bony shoulder. They rode one on either side of him. Even if he could have found the strength and will to try for a break, he was hemmed in with nowhere to go.

When they rode down the main street he could see that the changes at his home had not affected Shannon Plains. The town was as he knew it, as it had remained in his memory throughout the long war years and their aftermath. They rode past the offices of the *Shannon Sentinel*, and he caught a glimpse of the newspaper's editor, Sol Cain, heading up the street towards the Sunrise saloon. Becky Jones, the café owner, was older, her hair greyer, her smile still bright enough to light up the town as she watched them ride by.

She looked straight at Shannon, then nodded at Dancer and turned away.

But Billy Bedford, the town marshal, had been replaced by a new man. Tall and lean, with sunken cheeks and a sightless white eye, he stared dispassionately from his doorway at Shannon as they approached, then went back inside. Lancer and Dyson dismounted in front of the jail and tied all three horses. They unlashed Shannon's wrists, pulled him roughly out of the saddle and bundled him into the jail office.

The marshal was seated behind his desk.

'Caught him on the boundary of the Bamber spread,' Lancer said. 'A dead cow with its calf, a dying fire, a hot running iron.'

Dyson had brought the wrapped iron in. He dropped it with a thud on the marshal's desk.

A plaque on the desk bore the name Eli Simm. That said something about him, that plaque, Shannon thought. The marshal had an inflated ego. Fancied himself as some kind of superior lawman. Or maybe someone had instilled in him a disproportionate regard for his own self-importance. Someone like Jack Bamber.

'He's guilty of something,' Simm said, 'if that's what you found. But are you saying he's the one behind the rustling?'

The voice was deep, a voice from the grave.

'He's involved, that's all.' Lancer's tone was disparaging. 'If there's an organized band of

21

rustlers out there they'll be ramrodded by a bigger man than this drunken drifter. '

'I think—'

'Bamber doesn't pay you to think. Lock him up. Later, you can talk to Bamber.'

A faint flush was visible on the marshal's lean face. His lips tightened as he got out of his chair and reached up to a peg for a big bunch of keys.

Nobody's mentioned my name yet, Shannon thought as Simm ushered him out of the office and through to the cells at the rear of the jail. Lancer and Dyson want me locked up fast, a cattle thief with no name – so maybe this man isn't just an obedient puppet being jerked about by a powerful land baron – a land baron making illegal use of another man's property.

Yes, Jack Bamber surely was a crook, of that Shannon was certain.

Then he was pushed roughly into a cell. The door clanged shut. A heavy key turned in the lock. Through the bars, Shannon looked into the marshal's mismatched eyes, saw there bright intelligence and . . . what? Indifference? Distaste? Simmering anger at Deek Lancer's curt order?

'They didn't give you my name,' Shannon said.

About to swing away and return to the office, Simm sighed in obvious exasperation and said, 'But you're about to rectify that error.'

'Those two men picked me up on my pa's property. I'd rolled out of my blankets, smelled wood smoke and was looking at clear evidence of rustling.' He waited for that to sink in, saw no indication that it had, and said, 'My name's Frank Shannon.'

'Yeah,' Simm said, 'An' that makes you 'bout the sixth Frank Shannon to turn up since old man Shannon lost control of his ranch and rode off into the hills. Opportunists every one, and like all the rest of 'em – you're a phoney.'

'What d'you mean,' Shannon said, 'lost control of his ranch?'

'Maybe I should have said had it wrested from him. By Bamber. A powerful man who always gets his own way.'

'Not this time,' Shannon said flatly.

'Has so far,' Simm said.

'What about you?'

'I mind my own business, collect my pay, set back and watch everything in Shannon Plains runnin' real smooth. Right now I don't see Frank Shannon before me, I see a cheap cattle thief. That don't put you in a position from where you can begin rattling Bamber's chain.'

'Oh, I will,' Shannon said. 'The Slash S has been owned by my family for generations. You're telling me a brash Texan rode into town and took over Slash S; I'm telling you Slash S was founded by my grandpa, and I'll make damn sure it's returned to Tom Shannon.'

'First,' Simm said, 'you've got to get out of jail.'

That parting shot was fired over his shoulder as he went back into the office. The door clicked shut. Shannon was alone, a prisoner in a cell. And all he had to keep him company was a riot of bitter thoughts.

He took the couple of short paces to the iron cot, and sat down. The warming sun was slanting through the small, barred window. He could hear the clatter and hum of the town awakening and beginning the business of the day; the murmur of voices from the office, Simm's deep tones overpowering Lancer and Dyson's.

A good word, Shannon thought: overpowering. He had that sense of being overpowered by circumstances, yet he knew that if he was to sort out the mess he'd ridden blindly into he'd need to do some overpowering of his own. From a jail cell, that would prove difficult. But he had not made the decision to end his wandering ways and symbolically bury a shattered whiskey bottle only to have his future snatched away from him by a hard-nosed land baron.

He needed help – but where could help be found? So far he had glimpsed two familiar faces – newspaper editor Sol Cain, and the café owner, Becky Jones. The white-haired marshal who had been in charge when Shannon rode away to war had been replaced by Eli Simm – in Shannon's judgement he looked like a fence sitter, and fence sitters could fall on either side.

So Simm was a possible, someone to be worked on, worn down. Shannon reached into a pocket, rolled a smoke and fired up, then let his mind drift far and wide in its search for salvation. The wide sweep didn't bring much joy.

Closer to home, Shannon recalled the town's lawyer, Mack Findlay. Findlay had been his pa's closest friend – but, like the previous marshal, he had been getting old before the war. Would he, too, be retired?

It occurred to Shannon that if Findlay had still been in business, he would surely have done something to help Tom Shannon when Jack Bamber made his move. He also recalled that Bamber was a newcomer. Where had he come from? What drove him to the takeover of the Shannon empire?

All those questions stayed with Shannon, unanswered, through a long, wasted day. Meals were passed to him by a fat deputy. Simm popped his head around the door just once, late in the day, presumably to see if Shannon was still alive. He called 'Goodnight', but the question Shannon threw at him bounced off the office door as it slammed shut. And, when darkness began to fall, it was a determined Frank Shannon who sat hugging his knees on his cot. Simm had gone home. The fat deputy would bring him one last meal.

As night settled over the town, Frank Shannon

made a solemn vow that the supper the deputy was soon to serve would be Shannon's last in the jail. He was getting out, no matter what that took. And, once out, he would head for the cabin in the hills, talk to his father and find out the truth.

FOUR

'If that drifter really is Frank Shannon, then it won't be too long before somebody in town recognizes him,' Deek Lancer said. 'They do that, there's a can of worms open and wrigglin'.'

The Slash S bunkhouse was lit by a single smoking oil lamp. Jack Bamber was sitting with his elbows on the table close to the big iron stove. Across from him, Deek Lancer was smoking a battered cigarette. A whiskey bottle was at his elbow. He was looking at Cole Dyson. Dyson was lying on the cot closest to the table, fingers laced behind his head.

The rest of the room was empty. The oil lamp failed to throw light into the far corners. The room seemed to consist of nothing but that circle of light around the table, the stove, the bunk.

'We should have plugged him soon's we saw

him,' Cole Dyson said. 'He was caught cold with a running iron and evidence of rustling. One shot would have got rid of the problem, none of this would be happenin'.'

'You sayin' I done wrong?' Lancer said. 'You think maybe you should be foreman? You had the rifle up, a bead on the man: if you felt that way, all you had to do was squeeze the trigger.'

'What I'm sayin' is there was a way out and we didn't take it – for whatever reason. Dead men don't talk. People in town can't recognize a Shannon if he's twenty miles away and six feet under.'

'But he's not,' Jack Bamber said. 'He's in jail.' The lean man's eyes were empty. Deep in thought, he had no sense of panic. He'd stated facts: Shannon would be recognized, but he was in jail. Now he mulled over what he'd said, looking for ways in which the situation could ruin their plans; ways in which it could be manipulated for their benefit.

'Recognizing the man,' he said, 'doesn't change what happened. The Shannons are a spent force. A drifter stinking of raw whiskey was caught cold with a running iron in his hand and a cow with smudged brands; that drunken cattle rustler's been thrown into a cell. He'll hang, regardless of his name. If that man is Frank Shannon – so what?'

'What about Eli Simm?' Lancer said.

'Same answer. There's a town marshal got a rustler locked up in a cell. Simm'll do his job. The fact he works for me doesn't come into it.'

'It might,' Lancer said, 'when that old lawyer across the street hears who it is Simm's got in his jail.'

'Even that wily old-timer can't argue against the evidence of four honest eye-witnesses.'

Lancer's look was sceptical. He took a drink of whiskey, tossed the almost empty bottle to Dyson. The recumbent man drank it dry, coughed, with a flick of the wrist sent the bottle bouncing and skittering across the bunkhouse's dirt floor and into the shadows.

'You can stack your evidence a mile high, I still say we've got trouble a-comin' from Mack Findlay,' Dyson said. 'I never did trust Simm, and he'll be listening to some mighty persuasive arguments.'

'Trouble involving lawyers gets bogged down in talk,' Jack Bamber said. 'Always has done, always will. By the time the dispute digs itself out of the mire, we'll be long gone.'

'An' a whole lot richer,' Lancer said, and nodded his agreement. 'We rode up from the Big Bend to make a lot of money. I guess we've done pretty well up to now, got most of the way there. Now all we need is one big roundup and a drive to market, and we can kiss Slash S good-bye.'

He thought for a moment, his eyes on the glowing tip of his cigarette, then frowned. 'That drive to market's the big finish that'll wrap it all up all neat and tidy,' he said. 'It's the bonus, the icing on the cake – and I'm not sure getting rid of most of the hands was a good idea. It's not going to be easy taking cattle to market without the hired hands to drive them there.'

Bamber had risen from the table. He looked down the line of bunks, thought about what they'd set out to do, how they'd handled it so far – and nodded his satisfaction.

'I paid off the hands to save money. The forty and found that would have gone to twenty hands at the end of each month is safe in the bank. It'll end up in our pockets. And, no, a cattle drive won't be easy – but success or failure doesn't always depend on the head count; on how many cattle are in the drive. Quality pays. With the herd Shannon was building up, half a dozen men can take enough cattle to market to make a huge profit and substantially increase that bank balance—'

'Five men,' Lancer said. 'The three of us – and I can't see you working too hard. Plus Owen and Draper, the two you kept on the payroll.'

'All right, five,' Bamber said. 'Owen and Draper will play their part. . . .'

He deliberately did not finish, and there was a glint of cruel amusement in his eyes as he let his pause pack what was left unsaid with silent menace.

'What about at the end of the drive?' Cole Dyson said, his eyes on Bamber. 'Owen and Draper will have money owning to them. Do they get paid off?'

Bamber grinned. 'Oh, they'll get what's coming to them.'

Deek Lancer was also grinning. 'Whatever the hell that means.'

'I'd say we all understand exactly what's got to be done,' Bamber said, 'have done from the start, and that's why we're all going to end up rich men.'

With that he walked away from the table and out of the bunkhouse. As he crossed the yard he knew full well that Deek Lancer and his partner not only understood what was being said, but were already anticipating what had to be done. Owen and Draper were honest 'punchers who had been promised wages and a bonus. What they would get was a bullet in the back, a swift end to all their hopes and dreams.

Lancer and Dyson would willingly take care of that, because they knew it meant more money in their pockets. What they didn't realize, Bamber thought as he ran up the steps and crossed the gallery into Tom Shannon's house, was that only a fool split a big pot three ways when it was in his power to take the lot.

And with Owen and Draper out of the way and

the Slash S a distant and distasteful memory down his back trail, Bamber intended to take care of Lancer and Dyson.

FIVE

An oil lamp had been lit in the passage. At about ten o'clock that night the office door clicked open and the big deputy came through, carrying the tray. The dim light caused a man to look at things more closely, and Shannon knew at once that he'd been wrong: the deputy was not fat. He was one of those big men who are likely to turn to fat when age catches up with them but who, in their prime, can toss full grain sacks from barn to freight wagon without raising a sweat and see every small exertion add another ounce or two of rippling muscle.

And that change in his perception of the deputy, Shannon thought ruefully, meant the odds were stacked heavily against a successful jail break. But what did odds have to do with it? He had nothing to lose and, without the brains to control them, even the biggest muscles can be a handicap. *Especially* the big ones.

The trick was to turn the other man's handicap to your advantage.

A prisoner confined in a strap-steel cell could be fed only by unlocking the door and passing in the tray. This pattern had been established throughout the day. The first occasion had seen deputy and prisoner eyeing each other warily. The deputy had shown his astuteness by flashing Shannon a grin as he unbuckled his gunbelt and left it in the passage. Shannon had demonstrated his willingness to co-operate – or disinclination to cause trouble – by reclining morosely on the cot with his hands locked behind his head as the fat deputy placed the tin tray on the dirt floor just inside the door. The *muscular* deputy; who was clearly unfazed by entering the cell without his six-gun. Hell, Shannon thought, he could probably grab a steer by the horns and break its neck with a sharp twist of those powerful arms, so why should he be scared of an unarmed prisoner?

Which was precisely the thoughts Shannon hoped he'd planted in the deputy's mind by his meek and unthreatening behaviour. If he'd succeeded, then he'd lulled the big man into a false sense of security – and that could lead to carelessness.

All this flashed through Shannon's mind as the deputy came away from the still open office door, balanced the tray on one meaty hand and jangled the bunch of keys as he reached down to open the cell door. And Shannon allowed himself a small, inward smile. Both the deputy's hands were fully occupied. And this time he had left his gunbelt in the office.

Shannon watched the deputy like a hawk as the door creaked open. Rapid thinking could find no flaw in his reasoning as, through hooded eyes, he watched the man's movements: brains could outwit brawn; speed beat to the punch a strong man who moved ponderously. So Shannon again stayed on the hard cot, fingers laced behind his head. But this time there was a difference in his position. At other mealtimes, his legs had been stretched out, crossed at the ankles. Now his knees were drawn up. A small thing. Something the deputy would not notice. But it put Shannon in the right position to launch an attack – if the opportunity arose.

Maybe that chance wouldn't arrive on its own. Maybe, Shannon thought, leaving things to chance was expecting too much.

'Do me a favour, friend,' Shannon said, giving his voice a lazy, half-awake inflection. 'I've just got settled, so why don't you put the tray there on the end of the cot.'

It was late. The big deputy had been on duty most of a long hot day. He was tired, maybe smacking his lips at the thought of a long, cool drink before riding home and tumbling into the sack.

Thus preoccupied, he shook his head and said, pleasantly and without too much thought, 'Feller, if I wasn't in such a good mood. . . .'

He took those extra couple of steps from the place where he usually set the tray on the dirt floor to the end of the cot. He was tall as well as muscular. To put the tray down, he had to bend forward. He was slightly off balance. And he'd taken his eyes off Shannon.

With the speed of a striking snake, Shannon uncoiled. He rolled to his left. His left hand thrust down from the cot and its palm smacked the dirt floor. With his weight on that braced left arm his right leg whipped around in a ferocious kick. His booted foot caught the deputy behind his left ear. There was a sickening crack. The big man went down. Tin clattered as the tray shot high in the air then fell, scattering plate and food, hot coffee splashing from the tin cup.

The deputy rolled. Came to his knees. Shook his head.

Shannon couldn't believe what he was seeing.

He'd kicked the man so hard he thought he'd broken a couple of toes. But the deputy was already climbing to his feet. His heavy head turned. He looked at Shannon. His eyes were glazed, slightly crossed. But there was a smile on his face. He'd been here before, in a hundred knock-down, stomp-'em fights; mighty blows were there to be brushed off, just as formidable opponents would be brushed aside like annoying flies.

Shannon hit him again. He sank his fist into the soft flesh he knew he would find in the V of the deputy's ribs. His feet were spread and planted. He put his shoulder into the blow. His full weight followed through. In his mind he could see his knuckles slamming clear through to the man's backbone.

The deputy grunted. That was all. Then his left arm swung in a lazy, looping arc. A big fist connected with Shannon's cheek. It was like being hit by a blacksmith's hammer. Shannon was knocked sideways, away from the bunk. He hit the wall hard. His head felt loose. There was a high singing in his ears. He could see three oil lamps in the passage, all of them blurred.

The deputy glared at Shannon. One hand came up, absently rubbed the place behind his ear where Shannon's kick had landed. He looked at his fingertips, saw them stained red. With an angry exclamation he swung a foot and sent the tray clattering across the cell towards Shannon, stomped on the coffee cup, then turned towards the open door.

Shannon sucked in a hard breath. He saw the deputy's hand grasp the cell door, saw the bunch of keys still hanging in the lock; saw freedom slipping away. Then, cat-like, he scooped up the tray. He leaped across the cell and swung the tray sideways like a woodsman's axe. It took the retreating deputy at the base of the skull. His knees buckled. He sank heavily to his knees, one hand still clinging to the door. Bright red blood trickled down his neck.

Enough, Shannon thought. I hit him again, he's dead. He clamped his teeth. The deputy was still on his knees in the doorway. Shannon squeezed past him, brushed off a weak, restraining hand. Then he turned and with his foot pushed the big man off his knees and into the empty cell.

Now was the time for speed. The blow from the tray had done damage. The deputy lay where Shannon had pushed him. He was face down, his nose squashed against the packed dirt floor. One leg twitched – but that was all. But Shannon was aware of the man's strength, and he knew that one shout from the deputy would raise the alarm.

Shannon slammed the cell door, locked it, threw the keys across the passage. He went to the office door, cautiously poked his head through.

Empty. A lamp burning on the desk. A cup of coffee, steaming, an open sack of Bull Durham with tobacco spilling, the swivel chair's shiny seat awaiting the deputy's return. Across the room the street door was closed. Shannon's gunbelt dangled from a peg above a rack of rifles.

All this was taken in with one swift glance. Mere seconds passed. Behind him, he could hear the snuffle of the deputy's laboured breathing. To his front, the street was quiet: late night in a working town, few people about. There would be some hard-drinking souls propped up against the bar in the Sunrise Saloon – but to disturb them it would take a tornado, or a cattle stampede.

Shannon took down his gunbelt and buckled it around his waist, moved towards the street door. And all the time his thoughts continued to race.

The big deputy would recover fast. Shannon was in his home town, but he had last seen it seven years ago. Sure, it had appeared familiar when Lancer and Dyson brought him in, but that was nostalgia masking reality. Businesses would have changed hands, others closed, new buildings sprung up. Old names might have passed on. Friends would be few – or non-existent. He could probably find his horse – or any horse – in George Young's livery barn, but he was in enough trouble without adding horse theft and, if he had a mount, where would he go?

Would he, in any case, make it as far as the other side of the street if the deputy began hollering from the cell.

Shannon opened the street door, slipped through the opening onto the plankwalk and eased back against the wall. He was in shadow. The oil lamps lit the town only dimly. Pools of warm light fell on the plankwalk to spill weakly into the dusty street then fade away. Becky Jones's café was closed. Further up the street, brighter lights marked the Sunrise Saloon, and from there Shannon could hear the murmur of voices. Half-a-dozen horses were dozing at the saloon's rail.

His own horse had gone from the hitch rail outside the jail. It would be in Young's livery barn, across the street a short way up the slope. He could go there now, pick up his horse and ride out of town. But it wouldn't be too long, Shannon figured, before one of those men inside the saloon drained his final glass of beer and stumbled out through the door. If that happened when Shannon was stuck in no-man's land between jail and livery. . . .

Then, as his eyes moved away from the saloon, he noticed a light in a window almost directly opposite the jail and hope flared. Mack Findlay's office. The lawyer always did work late – but was he still in business, still *alive*?

It was a chance, Shannon decided. He could leap on his horse and leave town like the wind, but that's what Simm would expect. Instead, if he left his horse where it was, they'd be puzzled. And Simm would know Shannon might still have friends in town; friends willing to offer their help. As that possibility sank home, Shannon knew there was only one way to find out if that dimly seen oil lamp across the street was even now shining on the silvery hair of the Shannon's family's oldest friend and staunchest ally.

With one last, sweeping glance to left and right,

he pushed away from the jail's wall, stepped down into the dust and ran hard across the street. His boots thudded on the opposite boardwalk, matching the thumping of his heart. His eyes were drawn to the brass plate on the wall, and he bit his lip.

The name was unchanged.

Behind him he heard a faint shout.

Shannon sucked in a breath. He knocked sharply on the door. Without waiting for a reply he turned the knob and walked into the warm room as, in the cell at the back of the jail, the big deputy found his full voice and roared the alarm.

SIX

The man sitting at the desk was old and silver of hair, but the eyes that fixed on Frank Shannon were bird-bright. He seemed to take in the situation in that one sharp glance and, as the big deputy's bellows increased in volume, the lawyer put down his pen, pushed back his chair and stood up.

'Back room,' he said.

As he snapped his order, he leaned forward and blew out the lamp.

Suddenly the room was lit only by the weak light filtering in from the street. There was the stink of the smoke from the hot wick, then a sense of mustiness as the old man came away from his desk, plucked at Shannon's sleeve and led him through to the room at the back of the premises.

Shannon pulled the door to behind him. He stayed where he was, heard the whisper of sound as Findlay drew the curtains across the rear window. Then there was the scrape of a match. Light flared, another lamp was lit, and that was dimmed as the lawyer turned down the wick. In that wan light Shannon saw a table, several chairs, a wide dresser of dark wood, a makeshift bed covered tidily with grey blankets.

'Safe as we can hope for,' Mack Findlay said. 'If they knock, we don't answer.' He chuckled. 'But why should they? All I do,' he said, 'is fiddle around at that old desk in there. I'm a retired man, scratching pen on paper to keep memories alive.

'But you – what about you, Frank Shannon?'

In those first few minutes, all Frank Shannon was aware of was his own appearance. He had not shaved for several days. His clothing was trail worn. The stink of hard liquor was oozing from his pores, emerging with the sweat of fear and excitement to stain his skin like an incriminating brand.

And in front of him, sitting with his elbows on the table, was the man who, since his earliest recollections, Shannon had looked on with respect – because this was the man from whom wisdom and morality shone with an intensity equal to that of the disreputable aura in which Shannon was clothed.

Now, as he settled into a chair, he discovered that his thoughts had been read with amazing accuracy – but surely, from this man, that should have been expected?

'No man fresh out of jail looks his best,' Mack Findlay said. 'No man who arrives home to be branded a cattle rustler can be expected to understand, let alone accept, his plight.'

'I smashed the last bottle of hard liquor the minute I stepped onto Shannon land,' Frank Shannon said – and immediately wondered why.

'That sounds like a confession.'

'It's a commitment. I've taken my last drink. That was a vow I made before I rode into this situation. Now it holds even more firm because I've got me a mission.'

'Oh, that you have,' Mack Findlay said. 'And I hope to God the experience you've gained in your years away has equipped you for that task.'

'There could have been no better training ground,' Shannon said.

'But first,' Findlay said, 'you need to know what you've walked into.'

'Then someone must have pointed me in this direction,' Shannon said, 'because I know of no better man to tell the tale.'

'Even though I failed your pa?'

'There must have been good reason.'

Findlay sighed.

'I wish that were true. The only excuse I can make is that I retired from business a month before Jack Bamber moved in. I took a long trip to the east coast. When I got back your pa's spread had all been packaged and tied in a neat bundle by Bamber. Marshal Bill Bedford had gone, replaced by Eli Simm. Your pa was missing, along with your ma. He'd been sick for a while, running the spread down—'

'What, selling stock?'

'That, and laying off some of the hands. Kept two local boys on, Chick Owen, Phil Draper – they're still with Bamber, kept there with the promise of a big bonus.'

'For what?'

'You pa was cutting back, but also investing sensibly. He brought in an Aberdeen Angus bull for breeding. The stock he had was of vastly improved quality. It's been fattened up by Bamber.'

'Take 'em to market, he'll make a killing.' Shannon nodded. 'You say Pa was sick?'

Findlay spread his hands. 'Nothing you could pin down. He was becoming morose, withdrawn. That was some time before Bamber arrived. I think as he got older he was looking back over his life. . . .'

'And then everything bequeathed to him, everything he'd done of any value, was taken away from him,' Frank Shannon said. 'As easy as that. . . .' He snapped his fingers.

'And there wasn't a man in town,' Findlay said, 'could look me in the face and tell me how it had

45

all come about in so short a time.'

'The ranch deeds?'

'Signed over to Jack Bamber. Negotiated through a shyster lawyer who rode in with him and left town just as fast.'

'His financial status above board?'

'Bamber brought in no cash, no assets, nothing. Now his name's on the bank's documents as owner of Slash S, all the capital your pa had belongs to Bamber.'

'And you still don't know how this came about? Why my pa agreed to it – as surely he must have done?'

Findlay shrugged. 'I've got some ideas. But they're half-baked theories, no more than that.' His sharp eyes alighted on Shannon. 'My feeling is you should go out there with an open mind, see what you can dig up. Then we can get together again, see if what we've got matches up.'

'Difficult. I'm a man on the run.'

'Not a new experience, I'd guess,' Findlay said, and his eyes twinkled.

'Yes, I've been there, and handled it,' Shannon said. He took a deep breath, caught the liquid glint and noticed the whiskey bottle on the dresser, tore his eyes away. 'Now I've a damned good reason to do the same again.'

'They might let you alone. Bamber likes to think he runs a tight ship. Keeps things contained here in Shannon Plains. But maybe he wraps himself in illusions. If you stay out of sight, don't step on his toes. . . .'

'All right.' Shannon nodded. 'But if you can't give me the full story, you can at least tell me where to start.'

'Your pa. . . .' Findlay hesitated. 'He took it badly – whatever it was that happened.' He shook his head. 'You see? I'm as wise as you are – and, regarding this matter, I know you're about as wise as a dead owl. I think your ma is the person to talk to. I'm not saying she took it better than your pa or, if she did, that makes her a stronger person. What I suppose I'm saying is that your ma – because she married into the Shannon family – was not so weighed down by history. It wasn't your ma's parents who built up an empire, it was your pa's. Losing all that must have hit him hard. Perhaps too hard for a man to take.'

Again Findlay shrugged, and when he sat back Shannon could see that the old man was tiring, worn down by distressing thoughts and the lateness of the hour.

And it was then that a heavy fist pounded on the front door, rattling it in its frame.

'Findlay! You in there?'

'Leave them be,' Mack Findlay said wearily. 'They'll go away after a while.'

'Findlay! There's been a jail break. Rustler callin' hisself Frank Shannon.' A long pause. 'Nigh to killed Ed Baines with a goddamned meal tray' – Findlay flicked a glance at Shannon – 'then walked out the door. . . .'

The voice trailed away. More words were said, but the man was walking away from the door, talking to a companion. Retreating footsteps thumped on the plank walk. A horse whinnied.

'That was Simm,' Findlay said, and Shannon nodded. 'Someone must have come a-running when Baines hollered, found him, then roused the marshal.' He pondered for a few seconds, his lips pursed. 'If Ed could holler like that,' he said, 'he must be in better health than Simm suggests.'

'He's a hard man,' Shannon said, 'and I was lucky.'

But Findlay's thoughts had already moved on. He stood up, rail-thin but straight as a hazel sapling, came away from the table. Shannon rose, waited.

'I suggest you stay here for a while,' Findlay said. 'Get some shut eye, wait until the fuss has died down – but make sure you move out before dawn.' He hesitated, frowning. 'I'll walk out, lock the door. If I'm seen, if Simm tackles me, I'll say I was asleep when he knocked, ask him what the hell's going on.'

'Thanks,' Shannon said, and knew it was nowhere near enough.

'Your pa's living out near Cap Rock Gap. Don't expect too much.'

And then he was gone. The inner door closed

behind him. The street door opened and closed and a key turned.

Frank Shannon was enclosed in silence, alone with his thoughts.

SEVEN

For a time he dozed, stretched out on the cot in Mack Findlay's simple back room behind his office; awoke with a start, listened for a moment then lay staring at the ceiling in the light from the turned-down oil lamp.

He guessed Findlay stayed the night in this room from time to time. He'd already been a widower for several years when Shannon left town. With nobody waiting for him in his home it would be an easy decision to stay put after finishing whatever it was he did at his desk, and he could always ensure a pleasant drift into sleep with a couple of shots from the handy bottle of whiskey.

Shannon squeezed his eyes shut, blanked his mind to temptation.

He was suddenly aware of sounds out in the street: footsteps in the distance, low voices. So they were still looking for him. They'd have found his horse still where they'd put it in the livery barn, checked to see if any others had been taken and, after drawing a blank, would have figured correctly that he was still in town.

But finding him would be difficult. Nobody likes to be woken up in the dead of night and asked if they've got a rustler staying with them, so knocking on doors might be a last resort. Simm, or the big deputy if he was fit – what was his name, Ed Baines? – would try to put themselves inside Shannon's head, work out what he was most likely to do, where he was most likely to hide. But that could be anywhere. In town there were alleys criss-crossing on both sides of the main street, back yards a-plenty – a hundred and one places where a desperate man could make himself invisible until it was safe to move. On the outskirts of town there were trees and scrub where a man could bed down under the stars and stay pretty well hidden. From there, unable to be seen yet out in the open, it would be relatively easy to slip away unnoticed.

But when would that be possible, Shannon thought? And how much more difficult would it be from here, in the very centre of town? Then he took a deep breath, as he remembered the vow he'd made as darkness fell outside the barred windows of his cell. He had sworn to get out – and he'd done that. Then he would head for the shack in the hills, see his folks, and search for the truth. That was still ahead of him. He had completed half his task, but he had unfinished business. . . .

He tensed as footsteps drew closer – this time *behind* Findlay's premises. He twisted on the cot, looked at the window, satisfied himself that the curtains were fully closed; wondered if the material was thick enough to block the faint light from the lamp. Still half turned, his skin prickled as the back door rattled and somebody tried the latch. Just the one attempt. Then the footsteps scraped, and Shannon sensed that the searcher was now at the window.

Voices again. So there was more than one man. He thought he heard one say to the other that it wasn't the first time old man Findlay had left an oil lamp lit. That answered his questions about the curtains: the light was visible. But it didn't matter. Findlay was well known, these men were used to his odd habits. The voices faded, footsteps receded, and Shannon relaxed.

But only for a moment.

If any time was right to make a move, surely it was now. And, clearly, he should leave by the back door. It had just been checked. Attention would now be concentrated elsewhere.

With a decisive grunt he rolled off the cot. A swift glance at the lamp, then he decided to leave it lit; to leave everything exactly as it was. He checked his pistol, went to the back door. The key was in the lock. He turned it, eased the latch; pulled the door open a fraction and felt the inrush of cool night air.

Sounds seemed magnified. He could hear the two men away to his left. An alley ran behind the block of business premises. There were no backyards. If he did slip out, and the men turned to look behind them – he was dead. But what else could he do? Wait?

No. Shannon shook his head. There might never be another opportunity. Silently, he slipped through the narrow opening and pulled the door to behind him. Flattened himself against it. Looked left.

Two men. One probably Simm. The other almost certainly the big deputy, Ed Baines. Shannon had mixed feelings: he was relieved that the big man was on his feet, but wary: the deputy's strength and ability made him dangerous. Shannon had lured him into a trap, but that had been possible only because Baines been caught cold, taken off guard. Next time, he'd be ready.

A high moon floated in cloudless skies. It cast deep shadows. Emboldened by the conviction that he could not be seen, Shannon took a cautious sidestep to his right – and kicked a stone. The rattle was faint, but the sound carried on the thin air. It reached Baines's sharp ears. He stopped, touched Simm on the shoulder, looked back.

Shannon froze, held his breath. He knew that movement would give him away; that a man out in the open might remain unseen if he stayed absolutely still – and he was in shadow, against a dark timber wall.

For a long moment he thought Baines was not going to leave it; that he was about to come back. He braced himself, ready to turn in an instant and sprint away down the alley. Then he clearly saw the deputy's massive shoulders shrug, saw him shake his head. A whisper of sound: '*Must've been a rat . . . something. . . .*'

And then they were gone. They'd reached an intersection. They turned into it, making for main street and the jail. Shannon released his breath in an explosive gasp and began walking rapidly in the opposite direction. The alley sloped upwards. He was walking parallel to the main street, and knew that Young's livery could be no more than fifty yards away.

Would there be a back door? From hazy memories that were gradually revealing more and more he thought he knew the answer to that one, and when he'd covered those fifty yards the big double doors proved him right. He leaned a shoulder against them, aware of his pounding heart and dry mouth. There would be brackets inside, a beam that could be dropped into them to lock the doors. If that was in place. . . .

He curled his fingers around the edge of one door, pulled. It moved easily on oiled hinges. He felt a surge of relief. He stepped back, prepared to pull the doors wide – and stopped.

Marshal Simm would surely realize that sooner or later Shannon must try for his horse. If the lawman was worth his salt, he'd have a man stationed in there. His hand still on the door, Shannon thought for a moment, remembered the stumble that had almost betrayed his presence. He stooped, picked up two stones. He stuffed one into his pocket. Then he stepped back and hurled the other in a high arc over the barn.

There was a faint, muted thud, then a clatter as the stone rattled down the back of the barn's false front and fell onto the roof.

Swiftly, Shannon pulled the door open and slipped through the narrow gap into darkness and warmth and the smell of fresh hay and horses. One of the animals sensed or heard his arrival, and whickered softly.

Shannon closed the door, leaned against it, and stood perfectly still.

At the other end of the runway the barn opened onto the main street. There were no doors. In that wide opening a man was standing, silhouetted against the lamplight. He had a six-gun in his hand. He was looking upwards. His head moved from side to side. He glanced behind him into the depths of the barn, peered uncertainly into the darkness. Then he took several steps into the street, turned and looked up at the barn's high false front.

If Simm and Bains reached the main street and are heading this way instead of going back to the jail, Shannon thought, I'm finished. He waited, his back flat against the old timber doors, safe in the knowledge that he could not be seen, but tension hitting him so hard it was tightening his chest and making breathing difficult.

The man sent there to watch for him pouched his pistol and walked back into the barn.

Now what? Shannon's horse was there, somewhere – but impossible to get to without alerting the guard. Looking about him in the dim light, Shannon saw his worn saddle on a rail. His Winchester was still in the boot. Close, yes – but they could have been a million miles away. In any case, pistol or rifle, he could not risk the noise of a shot.

He chewed his lip, thinking. At the other end of the barn, the guard had relaxed and was leaning against the wall. He took out the makings, swiftly rolled a cigarette. The flare of the match lit the hard planes of his face.

Impatiently, Shannon surveyed the livery barn's interior. It had the usual row of stalls down one long wall, rails for saddles and equipment, pitchforks and shovels leaning against the walls, a broad runway sprinkled with straw – and a ladder leading to a square opening in the upper floor.

Not too far from where Shannon was standing. And he had another stone in his pocket.

Drawing a deep breath, he wrapped his fingers around the stone, inched his way out of the shadows – and stood still. The man sent to watch for him hadn't moved. He was smoking, looking towards the street. Shannon took another careful step. Then he drew back his arm and sent the stone flying through the open hatch and into the loft. Before it could fall and the sudden noise bring the guard's head snapping around he stepped back and was again lost in the darkness.

The stone clattered on the upper floor. The guard's head shot around, light glinting in his staring eyes. The six-gun flashed into his hand. He came away from the wall and started down the runway.

In his mouth the cigarette glowed. His eyes were narrowed against the smoke, fixed on the ladder. He reached it; reached up with his free hand to grasp a rung; hesitated. Then he placed a booted foot on the bottom rung and stepped off the floor.

Smoothly, silently, Shannon drew his six-gun.

Awkwardly, off balance because he was using just the one hand, the guard flattened himself against the ladder and lifted his foot to the next rung.

Shannon sprang out of the shadows. He swung the six-gun in a fast, whipping blow and struck the guard across the back of the head. The man grunted. Then he collapsed. His head hit the runway. The six-gun slid across the packed earth.

Frank Shannon stepped back, used his boot to grind out the man's smouldering cigarette. Then he took a deep, relieved breath and pouched his six-gun. It took him but a moment to locate his horse, a couple of minutes to lift his rig from the rail and saddle up, less than that to lead the horse into the moonlit alley and close the barn doors.

Then he mounted up. He took it slowly, picking out what soft ground he could find in the alley to muffle the sound of his horse's hooves. After thirty yards or so, he turned left down a cross-alley that took him away from the main street. In a little while he was clear of the town's business area. Buildings became fewer. He began passing small houses with gardens and picket fences, then others that were no more than falling-down tar-paper shacks on the very fringes of Shannon Plains.

And suddenly he was out in the open and bathed in clear moonlight.

With a swelling sense of relief that threatened

to burst forth in a roar of triumph – an instinctive, joyous cry he quelled with great difficulty – Frank Shannon put spurs to his horse, urged it into a gallop and headed for home.

EIGHT

He had been heading home for a long time, but the home he would reach within the next few hours would be very different from the warm image he had carried with him in his heart on the journey that had taken several years and covered many hundreds of miles.

It would not only be different, it would also be dangerous; going there at all would be risky, because it wouldn't take long for Marshal Eli Simm to figure out where the elusive rustler had gone. If, that was, he believed that the man he had thrown into a cell really was Frank Shannon. Even if he stuck with his belief that Shannon was just another in a long line of greedy impostors, he would come after him. Shannon had been caught, at dawn, with evidence suggesting he was behind the recent cattle rustling; he had assaulted a lawman and made a clean jail break.

All these thoughts troubled Shannon as he

pushed on across the flat land to the north of the town of Shannon Plains with his eyes squinting into the distance – but there was a potential problem much more worrisome than those he had left behind. The moon was fading as dawn brightened the eastern horizon. The brilliance of the rising sun was already casting a long, racing shadow before him, but it was also lighting the low-slung buildings of the Slash S. Ranch hands rose early.

To reach Cap Rock Gap and continue his search for the truth, Shannon was obliged to ride much too close to his father's sprawling ranch.

No, Shannon thought, it was not his father's ranch. In some weird way it had – according to Mack Findlay's story – been snatched from him in the space of probably no more than a single month. If there had been no whisper of violence, of coercion, then the transfer of ownership must have been done with his father's blessing. Yet how could that be? Why would a man who had inherited an empire from his father hand it over to a tall, rawboned stranger who rode in from nowhere and held out his hand?

The only explanation, Shannon decided, was that Jack Bamber was no stranger. Tom Shannon's pa had died when Tom was almost thirty. In his early twenties, Tom had spent a lot of time away from home before returning to settle down to life on the ranch that would one day be his and, somewhere down those old and twisting back trails, he and Bamber must have met. Collided. It was possible that out of some kind of explosive confrontation, Bamber had emerged the victor with a mysterious hold over Tom Bamber. Maybe over the years he had bided his time – maybe even half forgotten what had occurred such a long time ago. Then war broke out. Perhaps the man suffered losses, and in that suffering remembered the hold he had over a successful land owner. Again he waited. Until, with the conflict over, he reached the conclusion that in the aftermath of that terrible war all men would to some extent be weakened, and vulnerable.

And so he made his move and—

The crack of a shot jerked Frank Shannon out of his bitter reverie.

Deep in thought, he had ridden on without awareness or caution, and his horse had carried him too close to the Slash S.

A second shot came, the bullet humming overhead. When Shannon looked towards the ranch he saw two riders heading towards him at a gallop while, further back, a third man seated astride a standing horse looked at him along the barrel of rifle.

'Damn, damn, damn!'

With those muttered curses – placing the blame for his predicament squarely down to his own foolishness – Shannon put spurs to his horse and veered sharply onto a course that would carry him past Slash S's main gate and make the rifleman's next shot much more difficult. But the two riders spurring towards the entrance to Slash S were closing rapidly. Shannon recognized one of them as Deek Lancer. That suggested the rifleman was the blue-eyed Cole Dyson.

But the symbolic smashing and burying of the whiskey bottle was finally paying dividends. Freed from the brain-numbing effects of strong drink, Shannon's thinking was clearer than it had been for more than a year. As he stretched along his horse's neck and rode hard, he was weighing up his current situation with his earlier thoughts on Eli Simm. Drawing out Dyson and his companion had obvious advantages. If he could get away, then why not fool them into thinking he was heading back the way he had come and getting the hell out of Kansas? That message would get back to Simm, and to Jack Bamber at the Slash S. For a time at least, the heat would be off.

If he could get away!

A third shot cracked. Something plucked at his hat brim. Then the two men racing towards the gate opened fire with six-guns, and suddenly it was as if a swarm of hornets was buzzing around Shannon's head.

And still he was not past the gate.

Tightening his knees on the straining horse's

flanks, he reached down and slipped his Winchester out of its boot. He wrapped the reins around the horn in a loose half hitch, sat straight, and levered a shell into the breech. Then, twisting in the saddle, letting his muscles go limp to absorb the shocks from the horse's pounding hooves, he snapped a shot at Deek Lancer's horse. The bullet smacked home. Instantly, the horse's knees buckled. It went down hard. Lancer was flung clear. He rolled, then came slackly to his knees, shaking his head. The other man cast a final glance towards Shannon. A harsh curse rang out. He drew rein, looked back at the rifleman, and leaped from the saddle.

Riding like the wind, Shannon booted the Winchester, scooped up the reins and swept past the Slash S. His last sight of the two men was of Lancer shaking his fist after him as his partner helped him to his feet. Then he was clear and running, swooping down the trail along which he had been escorted by the Slash S hands, pushing hard for his overnight campsite close to the rustler's dying fire to give the clear impression that the man who had spent the night in jail was heading east, back to the border.

NINE

It was mid-morning when Eli Simm and Ed Baines rode up to the Slash S. As they cantered onto the spread Simm noticed the dead horse lying under the humming cloud of flies, and a short way further on the brass glitter of used shells in the short grass. He exchanged glances with the deputy. No words were spoken, but Simm knew that what he'd just seen had to be in some way connected with the man who had broken out of jail. From what Simm had learned, he knew there was only one place that man could be heading: Tom Shannon's place out at Cap Rock. To get there, he would have been forced to ride past Slash S.

In thoughtful silence the two lawmen rode the last hundred yards. They gave the mostly empty corrals a brief but critical glance, then they were over the hump and riding down the easy slope, past barns and trees and across the hard-packed yard to swing down in front of the house. The front door was closed. Simm hesitated, looked around. Then he saw Jack Bamber emerging from one of the barns and making for the bunkhouse. Simm turned and strode across the yard to intercept the lean rancher.

'I guess you don't need me to tell you that rustler got away.'

'Try pointing that out to Deek Lancer,' Bamber said. 'Your inefficiency damn near got him killed. He's down a good horse. The price of a new one should come out of your wages.'

He was talking without slackening his pace and, with a glance at Baines, Simm followed the tall man into the bunkhouse. Lancer was alone, sitting at the table drinking coffee. Bamber strode up the room's length and sat down across from the foreman. He reached over to the stove for the coffee pot, splashed the steaming black liquid into a tin cup.

Baines remained by the door. In the gloom the bandage on his neck was a startling white. Eli Simm walked slowly to join the two men at the table, sat down at what he considered a respectful distance. That thought gave him some amusement. Off hand, he couldn't think of anyone less deserving of respect than Jack Bamber. And he couldn't see how he was going to say what needed saying without risking an explosion of wrath from the lean man. Nevertheless. . . .

'It seems,' he said, 'that the man picked up for cattle rustling really is Frank Shannon.'

Bamber's lip curled 'Who's been talking? Some drunken bum up at the Sunrise?'

'Sol Cain. Frank Shannon's birth was announced in his newspaper twenty-seven years ago. Cain's watched him grow from boyhood to manhood and ride out to fight a war.' Simm shook his head. 'Becky Jones at the café is another. She recognized him straight off. There's no possible doubt.'

'Who he is changes nothing,' Bamber said. 'A rustler gets caught he hangs, whatever he's called.'

'Circumstances suggest a mistake's been made.'

Deek Lancer snorted, slammed down his tin cup. 'The mistake was Dyson didn't plug him on sight.'

'The man was returning home after seven years away,' Simm said. 'As far as he knew, he was on his pa's land. If he saw something suspicious, he'd investigate. That's what he was doing when your men rode out of the timber.'

Bamber sipped his coffee, seemed to be juggling with difficult thoughts. When he looked at Simm his gaze was cold. 'If he's Tom Shannon's son, he'll cause trouble.'

Simm met that gaze. 'You're the legal owner of

Slash S,' he said, and despite his efforts he was unable to keep the irony from his voice, or bite back a comment. 'Doesn't that make you untouchable. . . ?'

Ed Baines had been listening. Now he moved away from the door and into the room. He sat down on the edge of a cot. His movements were stiff. Deek Lancer was watching.

'Looks like your deputy got throwed by a wild bronc,' he said.

'Or got in the way of a desperate man who wasn't pleased with his accommodation,' Bamber said – and looked at Simm.

'I'm not condoning the man's actions,' Simm said, 'but I sure as hell can see why he was a mite riled.'

'Nevertheless,' Bamber said after a few moments' consideration, 'a man suspected of cattle rustling has attacked a deputy and broken out of jail.' He smiled icily at Simm. 'You're paid to do a job. Go after Shannon, throw him in a cell and hold him until the circuit judge arrives – then hang him.'

'Yeah,' Simm said thoughtfully, 'I can see how a man locked up in jail would have difficulty causing trouble.'

'Especially if you ensure there's strict control over visitors,' Bamber said, a faint flush colouring his lean cheeks. 'Lock Shannon up, throw away the key – and keep old Mack Findlay away from him. Understand?'

'If this feller's broken the law, I'll take him in. If he's Frank Shannon, and he's done nothing wrong, he goes free—'

'If he goes free, you're out of a job.'

'That's for the town council to put to the vote. And right now I'm in charge of law and order in Shannon Plains.'

'Then do your job,' Bamber said softly. 'There's a rustler on the run—'

'No. There's a man out there who says he's Frank Shannon. Witnesses confirm that. Before anything else, I'm after the truth.'

'I owe him no favours, but I'll go along with that,' Ed Baines said. 'But to get to the truth we've first got to catch up with the runaway.'

'If he is Shannon, he's gone lookin' for his pa up at Cap Rock,' Deek Lancer said. 'You want, I'll ride along with you, help you subdue him.'

'Difficult to do,' Simm said, 'when your best horse is out there feedin' the flies.' He noted the foreman's scowl, remembered the almost empty corral, and pushed away from the table. 'Anyways, we don't need you to point out where he's headed. And I reckon we've wasted enough time on pointless talk.' He looked at Bamber. 'I'll find Shannon, and I'll talk to him. If he can't convince me he's done nothing wrong, I'll make damn sure he stands trial; if what he tells me rings true, he goes free.'

And with that he gestured to Ed Baines and led the big deputy out of the bunkhouse and across the dry heat of the yard to their horses.

'What now,' Deek Lancer said.

Bamber was up and pacing, his lean face tight, his eyes blazing.

'Wait. Do nothing.' He cursed softly. 'Shannon will tell his story, Simm will believe you dragging him in at gun point was a big mistake, but that gives them nothing they can use against me.'

'We wait too long,' Lancer said, 'Frank Shannon will start digging deep, askin' questions. Maybe Tom's brain'll start workin', maybe he'll open up to his son, tell him how he lost Slash S.'

'What then?' Bamber stopped, hands on hips. Then he chuckled. 'Shannon's out there looking for the truth. Well, that's all Tom can tell his boy: the truth. And the truth is we rode into town and, in front of a lawyer, Tom Shannon handed Slash S over to it's rightful owner.'

'Is that what happened?' Deek Lancer said, grinning.

'Damn right it was,' Jack Bamber said, and the tension had gone out of his shoulders, the fury in his eyes replaced by cold calculation. 'And before too long Tom Shannon can take another ride into town and old Mack Findlay will sign the whole shebang back over to him – only by then we'll be long gone, and the mighty Slash S won't be worth a plugged nickel.'

TEN

Frank Shannon rode all the way to the creek bubbling by the cottonwoods where he had spent his first night on home territory, and there dismounted. He was quite sure he would not be followed. He left his horse to graze, built a small fire, and brewed coffee. As the sun rose and warmed the earth he sat back, rolled a smoke, and considered his situation.

His childhood home was owned by a stranger. He had been accused of rustling, thrown in jail, and escaped by assaulting a lawman. Old-time lawyer Mack Findlay had told him an unbeliev-able tale of opportunism and fast action by a man called Jack Bamber. But he had hinted that he, as the family lawyer, had his own ideas about what had happened. Shannon, on his way to find his father, had again fallen foul of Bamber's men. This time he had done some fast thinking and had – he hoped – bought himself some valuable time.

Time to discover the truth, from the man who had lost everything.

But how could he use it?

Findlay's suggestion was that he should 'go out there with an open mind, see what he could dig up'. 'Out there' being Cap Rock Gap, and the shack occupied by his ma and pa.

All right. That had been his intention. He had been diverted by a flurry of action, but intelligent thinking had seen him emerge from an awkward situation holding the advantage. Now he must make the most of it.

Decisively, Shannon ground out the cigarette, cleared the campsite and once more rode out.

This time, he headed north. In two hours of steady riding he pushed on across terrain that changed gradually from the flat, monotonous Kansas grassland to a landscape of low hills intersected by wooded valleys where fresh water tumbled over glistening rocks and birds soared lazily overhead against clear blue skies. There was no wind. Dust swirled at his horse's passing, hanging like a thin dun cloud in the hot, breathless air.

From time to time Shannon looked over his shoulder, but without too much concern. He had laid a false trail. No pursuit was expected, and nothing stirred on the vast expanse of flat land that lay behind him.

After a considerable time had passed he was able to make out the distinctive shape of Cap Rock in the distance, rearing high and shimmering in the heat. To one side of the mountain there was the pass known as Cap Rock Gap; somewhere below that – tucked away in the woods, Shannon guessed, close to fresh water and grazing – he would find the shack that Tom Shannon and his wife now called home.

Distance was deceptive, and it took Shannon another hour to reach the foothills. At once, as he turned off the short grass of the plain and put his horse to the slopes, the air became cooler, the grass underfoot green and moist. He had forgotten the name of the valley beneath Cap Rock Gap but, riding along the west bank of the meandering river, memory stirred and each twist and turn became suddenly familiar and he was transported back into a more pleasant past.

With predictable consequences. It was, it seemed, a recurring problem he would have to deal with if he was to survive; for when once again he came jerking back to the present and reality, it was to see yet another man with a rifle. This one was mounted on a grey horse. He was blocking the way forward. The rifle was aimed steadily at Shannon's belt buckle.

'My patience is being sorely tried,' Shannon said as he drew rein. 'Who the hell are you?'

'My question, I believe,' the stranger said.

'Frank Shannon.'

'Yeah,' the rifleman said, 'an' I'm President Ulysses Grant.'

'My pa's Tom Shannon. He owns Slash S. That makes me heir to the ranch he had taken away from him – temporarily.' He paused. 'If I'd been here, that wouldn't have happened. I aim to make amends.'

The young man watching him with disbelief written across his face was dark and stocky, like a chunk of hard wood sitting in the saddle. A Stetson was pushed back to reveal dark hair damp with sweat. Familiar, Shannon thought. I know this man – and even as the thought crossed his mind, he remembered the name. This was the boy born to lawyer Mack Findlay when he was in his sixties, a son of whom the old man was justifiably proud – but a son he had strangely neglected to mention when they'd been discussing the Shannon problems just a few short hours ago.

'You're Will Findlay,' Shannon said, and grinned at the sudden frown. 'You've changed some in the seven years I've been away – but I'm mortified that you don't recognize me.'

'Seven years back I was twelve years old,' Will Findlay said, and now his eyes were examining Shannon. 'I've grown up, but what the hell happened to you?'

'A long war and a disinclination to return

home until the devils eating away at my soul had been purged.' He saw the muscles along Findlay's jaw relax. The rifle was flipped up, then slid smoothly into its leather boot. Shannon said, 'I was talking to your pa, last night. He told me a strange tale, but made no mention of you, his son. . . .'

'Certain things are best left unsaid,' Findlay said enigmatically. Then Shannon saw him reach a decision. 'Come on, feller,' he said, 'let's go meet your family.'

It didn't take long. Will Findlay must have heard the sound of the approaching horse and ridden down to investigate. Now he made the return journey at a fast canter, and within half a mile Shannon could see the cabin set back against the timber, a small corral off to one side – the man sitting in a rocking chair on the wide gallery.

He moved his horse up alongside Findlay.

'What should I expect?'

The younger man shook his head. 'He's haunted by demons, much the way you must have been.'

'Does he mention me?'

'That's not for me to say,' Findlay said, and spurred away towards the corral.

It had been a long ride. He'd fought a war, crossed half a continent, and since hitting Shannon land he'd been jailed for crimes he'd not committed and been shot at more times than was comfortable. But the fifty yards from the creek – Sweetwater, hell, yes, that was it, Sweetwater Creek running through the valley with the same name – the fifty yards from Sweetwater Creek to the cabin were the hardest he had crossed in all that time, and their crossing took all of his courage. For the man he approached – white of hair, thinner than Shannon could have imagined possible – was staring into space with a gaze as empty as the limitless blue skies, and the approach of the man who was his son seemed to be making no impression on a mind that was someplace else.

'Pa.'

Shannon swung down; left the reins trailing; walked past the buckboard standing in front of the house and approached the gallery's rail.

'You took your time,' Tom Shannon said.

'There were one or two things that needed taking care of,' Frank said, and marvelled at the glib way he had dismissed a war.

'Yeah.' The squeak of a loose board, again and again. A booted foot pushed regularly. The chair rocked. The blue eyes turned to look at Frank, drifted away.

'But now I'm back.' Frank Shannon took a breath. 'I've already spoken to Mack Findlay. In town. We'll get things moving—'

'Roof needs fixin',' Tom said. 'A couple of

corral poles're loose, your ma needs—'

'I'm talking about Slash S. About getting it back. It's yours, Pa—'

'Your ma could do with a veg patch. We figured maybe over there, close to. . . .'

The words trailed away into silence. A hand lifted. A bony finger pointed, nowhere in particular. It was trembling – and Frank saw the glint of moisture in the old man's eyes.

'Pa,' he said hoarsely, 'we'll sort this out, take care of Bamber—'

'Frank!'

The shout dragged his eyes away, but not before he'd seen the jug standing on the boards close to his father's trailing right hand. It was the kind of jug familiar to moonshiners or those who dealt with them; a jug filled with the false hopes and empty dreams that are often the only refuge for lost souls.

Shannon took a deep breath and looked across the stretch of grass as once again his name was called. And now he saw there was another cabin, further along the line of trees. In front of it, Will Findlay was standing alongside a grey-haired woman who stood tall and straight and was beckoning furiously.

ELEVEN

'It's a place where we can talk without feeling those eyes on us,' Beth Shannon said. 'A man looking but not seeing, listening but not hearing. To see her man like that is enough to break a woman's heart. . . .'

They were at a table close to the window. Shannon was sitting across from his mother. Will Findlay was facing the window, bathed in noon sunlight. The room was snug, and obviously Findlay's: there was a stove, a cot, and everything about the place told of a masculine presence.

Before they entered the cabin there had been the greeting Frank Shannon had dreamed about on his long ride home: the warm embrace, gentle hands at his face, soft brown eyes devouring his appearance as if trying to make up in a single minute for everything missed during the past seven years.

Shannon had broken away first. He had been

uneasily aware of the shell of a man on the other cabin's gallery; aware too that Marshal Eli Simm would not be fooled for too long by the false trail Shannon had laid. With pursuit a very real possibility, Shannon had fed and watered his horse then taken it, not to the small corral where several horses dozed, but to a clearing a little way into the woods. It was tethered, but could move freely, and it had a supply of fresh oats. Out of sight, but within easy reach – and this smaller cabin had a back door.

Now it was down to business.

'All I know,' Shannon said, 'is that Jack Bamber arrived in Shannon Plains and wound up owning the whole shebang. In the space of a month.' He shook his head. 'How could that happen – and how can what happened be undone?'

'He came out to the ranch one evening,' Beth said. 'Your pa took him into the office. They talked well into the night, then rode to town. Bamber had brought a lawyer with him—'

'From where?'

Beth shrugged. 'Texas. Big Bend country. Who cares? What matters is they broke into Mack Findlay's office—'

'They *what*!'

Beth nodded, her face tight. 'Broke in, sprung the file cabinet, got out the Slash S deeds and everything was signed over to Jack Bamber. Marshal Billy Bedford was witness – his last official task before he got fired and Simm took over.'

'Pa was back East,' Will Findlay said.

'Yeah,' Shannon said. 'He told me that much, but I guess he was holding a lot back.'

'I've been trying since then,' Beth said, 'to get some sense out of your pa. But he's been beating a gradual retreat into himself until what you see now is all that's left.'

'Never any suggestion as to how or why Bamber could do what he did?'

'Nothing.'

Shannon looked at Findlay. 'Will, your pa told me he's got some half-baked, outlandish ideas about what might have happened. Has he said anything to you?'

Findlay shook his head.

'All right, so what about you?' Shannon looked enquiringly at the dark-haired youngster. 'What are you doing here?'

Findlay grinned. 'You remember this valley?'

'I do now – some; but what exactly are you getting at?'

'A couple of miles further on,' Beth said, 'it narrows down. At first glance all you can see is the river getting pretty wild, tumbling over rocks, steep slopes on either side and tall timber sort of pushing down real close to the water. . . .'

'But there's a way through,' Findlay said, still smiling. 'And beyond that narrow section the valley widens. There's rich pasture back there, in a natural basin that catches the sun and keeps out the worst of the wind . . . a fine place for cattle. . . .'

'Slash S cattle,' Shannon said softly. 'You're stealing stock. You realize you almost got me hanged?'

Beth's eyes widened. Shannon reached out, stroked her hand.

'Someone left a running iron by a dying fire. . . .' He looked at Will, saw the nod, the shamefaced look. 'I was caught, taken in.' He shrugged. 'It's a long story, but you haven't answered my second question, Ma.'

'What was it – how can what's happened to your pa be undone?'

Shannon nodded. 'Not just to Pa. To us, to a lot of good people.'

Her grey eyes were sad. 'It can't, Frank. So what we do is start over again, here in the hills, using stock that's rightfully ours.'

'How many head?'

'Fifty, so far,' Will Findlay said.

'What brand are you using?'

'S slash F.'

Shannon tightened his lips. 'And Pa doesn't know?'

Beth shook her head. 'He sits there every day. From time to time, Will brings cattle through, a few head. Tom sees them – must do.' She shook her head. 'Who knows what goes on in his mind?'

For a few minutes there was silence, that last question hanging like a pall. Will pushed away from the table and went outside. Beth seemed to be lost in thought, as if what had been openly discussed – perhaps for the first time – had suddenly brought home to her the hopelessness of their situation.

Because it was hopeless. To Frank Shannon it was clear that discovery was inevitable – and in any case, a ranch founded on herds of stolen cattle could never succeed. Taking those cows to market was bound to raise suspicion. But – hell, there were too many ways to slip up, the penalties too severe to contemplate.

'The wrong done to Pa must be undone,' he said quietly. 'We can't hide in the hills, forever tending stolen cattle.'

'What if the transfer of power was justified? What if something that looks like a wrong is actually right and proper and legal?' Beth was watching him, watching the effect of her words.

'How can that be?'

'There was a lawyer present: deeds were handed over.'

Again the shrug, as if she was deliberately waiting for her son's mind to start working. But Shannon was at a loss.

'If there's that doubt, then we ask Pa,' he said. 'We make him tell us what went on, why he willingly gave up a dynasty.'

Beth shook her head. 'You're wasting your time.'

'Then we go to Mack Findlay, ask him to explain his half-baked theories and see what we make of them; see if anything he comes up with makes sense.'

While he was talking, Will Findlay had slipped back into the cabin. There was a smile pulling at his lips, excitement sparkling in his eyes.

'Do it now,' he said, 'before it's too late. Eli Simm and that big deputy have just rode up to Tom's cabin. I guess it didn't take them too long to figure out where you'd be – and they didn't bother with a posse.'

'Oh God!' Beth said.

'Easy now,' Frank Shannon said. He rose from the table without haste, leaned across to kiss his mother's cheek, then nodded to Will.

'Step outside, wander over there and keep them occupied.'

'A job I do real well,' Findlay said, and Shannon knew the youngster was referring to the fifty head of stolen cattle grazing almost under the noses of the visiting lawmen and the times he must have talked his way out of trouble.

Then Shannon moved.

He stepped out of the back door, saw the dark of the woods almost up against the cabin's back wall and slipped silently into their cool shelter.

Voices drifted to him as he stood on a carpet of

needles in the dappled gloom. He heard Will Findlay laugh, the rumble of a deeper voice that would be Ed Baines; the peculiarly brittle tones of the marshal, Eli Simm

With a last glance in that direction, which told him nothing other than how well he was hidden, Shannon pushed up the slope through the trees. It was a short walk to the clearing. Within minutes he was mounted and walking his horse in a circle to the west that took him around easily and without incident to the mouth of Sweetwater Valley.

He was still hunting for the truth. The man he had expected to talk to him was frail of body, broken in spirit. All right, now it was time for the old lawyer to come clean, to spill what he knew.

One way or another, Frank Shannon vowed, one damn way or another he was going to find out what had happened when Jack Bamber rode in from the Big Bend country and destroyed Tom Shannon's world.

The ride into Shannon Plains took less time than the trip out to Cap Rock because Frank Shannon threw caution to the winds, cut across Slash S land and again rode past the big gate. This time no shots whistled past his head, no horsemen spurred towards him, there was no call for a frantic ride to carry him out of danger. Instead he let his horse bear him the rest of the way into town at a leisurely gait, hit main street at about four o'clock and, knowing that both lawmen were out of town, rode boldly down the centre of the street.

Again dismissing any thought of caution – but this time it was a bad idea.

As his horse kicked up dust on its way past the jail, Shannon saw a deputy lounging in the doorway. It was the man who had kept watch in George Young's livery barn, and he was watching Shannon closely. Few strangers passed this way. Shannon was all too aware of his unkempt appearance and – courtesy of Marshal Eli Simm – this man was sure to be carrying in his mind a rough description of the escaped rustler. But if he put two and two together and came up with the right answer, what would he do? Watch and wait? Or act?

Shannon had planned on hitching his horse to the rail closest to Mack Findlay's office and walking straight in to see the old lawyer. But the observant deputy brought about a swift change of mind. Instead, he rode on up the street then swung in through the wide doors of George Young's livery barn.

It was light, airy and empty. Shannon swung down, thought about unsaddling, and hesitated. There were several ways things could go wrong. The deputy could walk over from the jail and ask awkward questions. Simm and Baines could come hammering back into town at any time, their trip out to Cap Rock unfruitful. Between those two possibilities lay the threat posed by Slash S riders, Deek Lancer and Cole Dyson – and if Shannon found himself in a menacing situation, the last thing he wanted facing him was a horse with no saddle.

He was still wavering over what to do when George Young strolled in from the adjoining lean-to premises he called office and home. The one-time wrangler had been old when Shannon went to war. That put another seven years onto his age, but the wiry old-timer walked straight and tall, his shaven pate glistened like polished mahogany in the late afternoon sunshine. In the sharp grey eyes that settled on Shannon there was instant recognition.

'Dang me,' he said, 'I've caught me a rustler.'

'Hello, George,' Shannon said.

The old man's handshake was firm, his palm calloused.

'You rode in to give yourself up?'

'What do you think?'

Young chuckled. 'I think if you're back home to stay and are now figurin' on some Bamber hunting,' he said shrewdly, 'you'd best watch your step.'

'That deputy any good?'

'Cy Kenny? He's pure poison.'

Shannon pulled a face. 'Last night I came out through Mack Findlay's back door and in through yours. I need to talk to Mack. What do you recommend?'

'I'll wander over to the jail, keep that deputy talkin'. You take the same path you trod last night.'

Shannon smiled and nodded his thanks. 'I'll leave my horse saddled, close to the back door.'

'Tie him to a post,' Young said. 'We could do with some air, so leave those doors wide.'

He cuffed Shannon's shoulder, then swung away and walked nimbly out to cut across the street towards the jail. Shannon watched the old wrangler go and shook his head in wonder. He led his horse down the runway, hitched it to a post, found a bucket, filled it with water from the trough and placed it close to the horse. Then he swung the back doors wide and stepped into the alley.

Daylight had shortened the distance. But finding the barn in the dark had been easier than locating Mack Findlay's back door. Shannon walked briskly, approached the intersection taken by Simm and Baines and realized he'd gone too far. When he retraced his steps it was to discover that the crafty old lawyer was already ahead of him. His back door was now open, the old man waiting.

'Saw you ride up the street,' he said, 'so I figured it wouldn't be too long before you came calling.'

'The story you told me was full of holes,' Shannon said, as he followed the old man inside and through to the office. 'You knew damn well I'd be back to see them filled in.'

The curtains were drawn across the street window. The room was dim and cool. Findlay sat down behind his desk, gestured to a chair. Then he reached down, slid open a drawer and came up with a whiskey bottle. He lifted his eyebrows questioningly.

Shannon shook his head. 'The craving I had is dead and buried.'

'Then the extra measure you've passed on will help to warm an old man's bones,' Findlay said, and he poured generously into a glass and corked the bottle. 'So, what do you mean, full of holes?'

Feeling lost and at a disadvantage in a deep leather chair, Shannon frowned.

'Omissions,' he said. 'If I've been out to Cap Rock, then you know I've talked to your boy.'

'Will's helping them up there, yes, has been since this trouble began. His mother died when he was toddling – but of course, you know that – so he lives up there, eats well. I believe he has his own cabin.'

'Mm. You know anything about the S slash F brand?'

'I know Beth's set her mind to building a herd. How far they've got towards that doesn't concern me too much.'

He doesn't know, Shannon marvelled. The old man has no idea his son's involved in rustling Slash S cattle.

'So why's Will helping out at Cap Rock? What is it? Is it guilt?'

Now Findlay frowned. 'Will's – or mine?' Then he shrugged. 'Perhaps you're right. Guilt – because I wasn't here to do something when your father was being taken apart. Guilt because—'

'Because you've got those half-baked theories that are surely better than no theories at all,' Shannon said, 'yet you persist in keeping them to yourself.'

'Persist?' Findlay's smile was wry. 'You heard mention of those theories late last night. If I said no more then, that's hardly keeping a stubborn silence.' He swirled the whiskey in the glass, stared down at it, pursed his lips. 'Besides,' he said, 'what gives me the right to hear an old friend's secrets, in confidence, then pass them on to the first drifter to hit town?'

And now the old eyes twinkled with amusement, and Shannon was forced to accept the logic in the old lawyer's words – and smile grudgingly.

'I think,' he said, 'I'll have that drink after all.'

'It always saddens me,' Mack Findlay said, 'that a man learns more about his family's history from other people than he ever does from his parents.'

Shannon thought about that. Then he said,

'Maybe I left home too soon to be told, got back when it was too late for the telling.'

'You were twenty when you went to war. Will's nineteen now, and he knows all there is to know about every damn Findlay I can remember.'

'That's to your credit,' Shannon said. 'But what I'm interested in is the truth about what happened here. My father's a broken man. I aim to put that right, give back to him everything Bamber took away.'

'What I'm about to tell you could well have the opposite effect,' Findlay said.

'Then get on with it,' Frank Shannon said, and he took his first strong drink since his ritual burying of the whiskey bottle.

Findlay sat back in his chair, stroked his chin with a mottled hand. 'Tom Shannon, your father, was the younger of two brothers,' he said. 'His father – your grandpa, Jesse Shannon – always favoured his first born. Unnaturally so. And that boy made the most of it. If Tom had anything and the elder brother wanted it – he got it. With his father's approval and, if necessary, his connivance. If Tom wouldn't give up whatever it was the other boy wanted – perhaps even Tom's most treasured possession – he was dragged to the wood shed and beaten with a strap. When that had happened several times, he had learned a hard and painful lesson.'

There was a sombre silence. Frank Shannon

again tasted his whiskey, this time felt instant repulsion and grimaced as he leaned forward to put the glass on the end of the desk.

Findlay was watching him, but his mind was on other things.

'I remember,' he said, 'Tom told me how his brother took away the first pistol he ever had. Jesse gave them both a weapon of some kind when they reached fifteen. The elder boy got an old hunting knife. When Tom reached fifteen he got a Collier flintlock pistol, converted to percussion.' He shook his head. 'His big brother wanted it, he took it – and Jesse laughed when Tom complained.'

'What about his mother – my grandmother, Ruth Shannon?'

'A woman could do nothing while she lived in that man's house. So she did the only thing her husband could not prevent: one dark night when Jesse was too drunk to stand, she took the buckboard and drove away. She walked out on him. The *elder* son went with her willingly – he was seventeen then, a couple of years older than Tom. And he went because, despite taking full advantage of his father's favouritism, the obvious injustice of it had instilled in that boy a contempt for his father; Tom's father; your grandpa, Jesse Shannon.'

'I can't see where this is heading,' Frank Shannon said. 'My pa was treated badly, his mother left home with Tom's brother. . . .'

'They moved down to Texas, your mother and the boy,' Findlay said, and he allowed himself a thin smile as Shannon tensed. 'Down there – the Big Bend country, I think it was' – he saw Shannon's quick nod – 'Ruth Shannon took up with another man. A good man. She lived with him for the rest of her life but, because she was still married, she did not, *could* not take his name. However,' Findlay said, 'Tom's brother *did* take that good man's name.'

And the lawyer left it there. The room was enveloped in a silence that seemed to deaden even the faint sounds that filtered in from the street. In the dim late afternoon light that seeped in through the curtains the old lawyer's eyes were strangely luminous – and they were fixed intently on Frank Shannon.

'Yeah, I can see it now,' Shannon said. 'That good man's name was Bamber, wasn't it? The elder brother's name was Jack, and I guess that explains why my pa handed over the Slash S.'

'Force of habit,' Findlay said. 'A lesson learned painfully in childhood and never forgotten.'

'Perhaps not,' Shannon said. 'There is that, of course – but when it all boils down, who was the rightful heir?'

'The elder brother.'

'So, just like my ma suggested, justice has been done.'

'I don't know,' Findlay said, and his sudden smile was enigmatic. 'And neither do you.'

Shannon frowned. 'But . . . the story you've just told—'

'I made it up.'

'You *what*!'

'Oh, it was true enough up to a point. Tom's childhood was as bad as I described it; his mother walked out with the elder brother; they were believed to have moved down to Texas.' He sipped his whiskey, his eyes twinkling. 'The rest of it . . . well, that was neatly told so that you could jump to the obvious conclusion.'

'But if the elder brother's name was Jack—'

'It wasn't. Or, not exactly. Tom's brother's name was John.'

'Close enough,' Frank Shannon said softly, pensively.

Dusk had fallen. The office had become uncomfortably gloomy. Mack Findlay reached for matches and lit the lamp. Shannon left his chair and moved to the window, pulled the edge of the curtain aside and looked out. He could see across to the jail. The door was closed. Only one horse dozed at the rail.

He let the curtain fall, moved away from the window with his mind in a whirl. He sat down on the edge of the chair, tried to concentrate.

'Mack,' he said, 'what you've come up with is a logical reason for my pa to give up his ranch, based on the story he told you about his child-hood, about his brother. But too much of it's conjecture. The man out there on Slash S is called Jack Bamber – and that's a long way from John Shannon.'

'Indeed. So come up with a better theory.'

'I can't.'

Findlay shook his head. 'Neither can I – and, apart from Bamber, there's only one man around who can tell us if I'm right.'

While they were pondering on that indis-putable fact in a heavy silence, they both heard the drum of hooves. They pounded up the street, the noise swelling. Shannon guessed four horse-men, maybe more. Suddenly, without conscious thought, he was struck by a terrible foreboding. He knew with absolute certainty what was happening. With a sharp glance at the old lawyer he sprang from his chair and again went to the window.

He'd been wrong about the numbers, but right in his instant sense of something being terribly wrong. Again he looked across at the jail, and now there was a swirl of movement as three horses swung in to the hitch rail alongside the deputy's horse. Eli Simm and Ed Baines dismounted. The big deputy went to the third horse. The man in the saddle was stocky and upright, but his hands were bound in front of him and a taut rope under the horse's belly was lashed to his ankles.

The big deputy stooped, slashed that second rope. Then he reached up and helped the man to dismount.

As his boots hit the dirt, the man with the bound wrists cast a glance across the street. For an instant his face was clear in the lamplight. Then Baines wrenched him around, bundled him up onto the plank walk and the three men went into the jail.

The door closed, the sound clearly audible in the office.

Shannon turned away from the window. Something in his face registered with Findlay, and the old lawyer's fingers trembled as he reached for his glass.

'It's Will,' Shannon said. 'Eli Simm's brought him in with his hands bound and taken him into the jail.' He saw the whiskey glass pause on its way to the lawyer's mouth, saw the sharp eyes become distant as Findlay's mind took in the information and began calculating the whys and the where-fores.

'Working out what's been happening to my pa was always going to be a tough chore,' Shannon said. 'If you think about it you won't have too much trouble understanding why your boy's been thrown into a cell – but getting him out again is going to test your lawyer's skills to the limit.'

TWELVE

Frank Shannon left town by the same route he had taken the night he broke out of jail. This time he was confident he would not be seen. Marshal Eli Simm was at that moment tied up talking to Mack Findlay who had crossed the street in the role of aggressive lawyer coming out of retirement. George Young had kept watch from the street as Shannon mounted his horse, and he waved a cheery 'all clear' as Shannon rode out through his livery barn's back door.

Despite his easy leaving of Shannon Plains, Frank Shannon rode hard towards Cap Rock with yet more ominous possibilities looming before him. Simm and Baines would have been forced to pass the Slash S on the way into town with their prisoner. Common sense suggested Simm would have paused long enough to tell Jack Bamber that his rustler had been caught. If so, Bamber would waste little time sending ranch

97

hands out to Sweetwater Valley to recover the stolen cattle.

For such a task, it was Shannon's belief that Bamber would rely on Deek Lancer and Cole Dyson. There was no telling what those two men would do now that they knew who'd been stealing Bamber's cattle. Shannon aimed to get to Sweetwater Creek before them, be there when they arrived to protect his elderly parents.

Shannon's horse had been ridden hard for several days. It was feeling the strain. Several times on the ride its rider was forced to ease back for the tiring horse to recover, and so it took him much longer than he had expected. And he was fretting with impatience. He had no idea if Beth had other hands out there helping Will Findlay. It had been Shannon's impression that Findlay worked alone. His discovery of the dying branding fire and the abandoned iron on his first day on home range seemed to bear that out.

That left his mother alone with Tom. He wasn't sure how either of them would cope with the loss of Will Findlay, or a visit from the menacing Slash S riders.

After an hour's riding, full darkness had fallen. Shannon was again forced to slow the pace. A short while after that the moon floated into cloudless skies and the way ahead became clearer. As if appreciating the pure light, the weary horse lifted its head and pushed on with renewed vigour. Cap Rock's peak was already visible, an eerie monolith rearing into the night skies. Before too long Shannon reached the point where he must turn off the open range and begin the ride along Sweetwater Creek – and at once he knew something was wrong.

He had been smelling woodsmoke for some time, but that was only to be expected: he was nearing his destination, both cabins in the valley had iron stoves for cooking and heating, and smoke would carry on the cool, clear air. But now, as he eased his mount carefully along the creek's uneven bank with the water gurgling and tumbling to his right, ahead of him Shannon could see a ruddy glow. Even as he watched, a brilliant shower of sparks rose high into the night air. He sensed, rather than heard, the fierce crackle and hiss of the intense blaze.

Then he was out onto open ground again and across the stretch of sloping grass now lighted by dancing flames he could see that the shower of sparks had been thrown high as the roof of Will Findlay's blazing cabin collapsed. On the gallery of Tom Shannon's cabin, two figures stood close together, their faces lit by the flames.

Grim-faced, Shannon held back for a moment, then spurred his horse up the slope. As he drew nearer it was like riding into a wall of heat. Tom and Beth had drawn back, and were standing on the far end of the gallery. The roar of the fire was deafening. Beth had her hands to her ears, and as Shannon watched she turned away from the terrible sight and pressed her face against Tom's chest. His big hand was on her back, stroking, stroking. His eyes were looking over the top of her head. It was as it he was spellbound, unable to comprehend the enormity of what had happened – perhaps even fully understand.

Casting a quick glance up the valley to the narrow section where the trees dropped down to the creek, seeing no movement there, Shannon swung out of the saddle and mounted the broad gallery.

'Ma.'

Beth started, and turned. When she saw Shannon, her face lit up for an instant. Then she shook her head, moved gently away from Tom.

'Simm came after you left,' she said, her voice raised. 'Baines was with him. He rode on up the valley, came back with a tale to tell. Then they took Will.'

'And this?' Shannon gestured at the burning cabin.

'Slash S men. Lancer, Dyson. They came later. Both of them are up there now. They'll be bringing the herd through, hoping to get it back to Slash S while the moon's up.'

'And how are you, Pa?'

Shannon was watching Tom. It was a question asked without thought, but in unnatural times people act in strange ways. And despite everything, the question was valid: in Tom Shannon's eyes there was the faint but unmistakable flicker of returning life; catastrophic events that would have left a normal man stunned were dragging his haunted mind back from its dark refuge. He was becoming *aware*, with that returning awareness there was anger – and Frank Shannon knew, instinctively and with a fierce surge of emotion, that he had done this; his father's sudden improvement was a direct result of his only son's sudden homecoming.

'My thinking sure is clearer,' Tom said, his voice creaking and still hesitant. 'But that doesn't help any of us. What's done is done, there's no going back to what . . . to what. . . .'

Knowing Tom wasn't talking about the fire, Frank Shannon said, 'Maybe I can make a change, put everything right,' then winced as his mother gripped his arm fiercely.

'No.' There was finality in Tom's dull tone – but his eyes were still alive, and he seemed to be watching and waiting for Frank's reaction; maybe – and Frank thought this was a real possibility – maybe deliberately prodding his son, pushing him to make himself clear and explain exactly what he meant by 'putting everything right'.

'Come inside the house,' Frank Shannon said.

'Tell me exactly what happened when Bamber hit town, let's see what we can work out.'

'No, that comes later,' Beth said. 'Those fellers, Lancer and Dyson, they'll be coming through with the herd, they'll see your horse. Move it now. You and your pa go on into the woods. Talk, if that's what you want, but keep your eyes open, and stay there till I call.'

Even as she gave the order, Shannon heard the drum of hooves. Then, out of the wooded path along the creek, cattle came trotting. Heads tossed. Rolling eyes were as luminous as those of wild animals in the light of the fire. Steers and cows snorted as they ran. They came thundering along a well-worn path, given their heads by the two Slash S riders who must surely be bringing up the rear. And, if Mack Findlay was right, these were valuable animals, sired by an Aberdeen Angus, beef on the hoof that would be sold for a high price at market.

But this was no time to admire the fruit of his father's labours. It was time to move.

'Get Pa out the back way,' Shannon said to Beth. Then he jumped down from the gallery and ran to his horse. He flung himself into the saddle, spurred up the slope and around the cabin. In the shelter of the high trees he drew rein. He leaned down, with his hand calmed the excited horse, reached to cup its muzzle and stifle the slightest sound.

Tom Shannon came stumbling out of the back door. Frank called softly. Tom ran over, grasped Frank's bent left arm and was swung up behind the cantle. With his father's strong arm around his waist, Shannon moved his horse off into the trees at a walk.

'Go right,' Tom said. 'There's a gap. We can see what's going on.'

And there was. Between the two cabins, a tongue of treeless ground poked into the woods, a pile of sawn logs at its head. Shannon drew rein in deep shadow, swung from the saddle behind the high stack of logs and waited for Tom do the same. Then, safely under cover, they watched as below them the cattle streamed by along the moonlit creek.

Will Findlay had been about right in his estimate. Shannon reckoned just over fifty head, every one of them padded with firm flesh – and when the last, slower animal came trotting out of the trees, it was followed by Deek Lancer and Cole Dyson.

'Give me your rifle, Son,' Tom Shannon said. 'I'll rest the barrel on that wood pile, drop both of them in their tracks.'

'All that would do is bring Eli Simm back, this time with a posse.'

'Simm won't know.' Tom's grin was wild. 'Hell, *nobody'll* know.'

'Maybe so, but killing those two men won't get

you the Slash S.'

But Tom was off, his mind drifting. 'Isn't that my herd?' he said falteringly. 'I gave no instructions. Where's Matt taking it?'

Matt. That was Matt Long. He had for many years been Tom Shannon's foreman, but had retired long before the war.

'Somewhere safe, where there's better grazing,' Frank said, watching Tom, knowing that there was no better grazing than the land along Sweetwater Creek – waiting for his pa to jump, to point out scathingly that Frank was talking nonsense. But no criticism came. Tom was frowning after the cattle, shaking his head. And Frank said, 'Matt knows what he's doing. Let them go. When they're clear we can settle down, do some talking.'

'I get tired,' Tom said. 'Talking . . . thinking. . . .'

'Then we'll take our time. There's no hurry. . . .'

The last of the cattle had moved out of the area of grass lit by the still crackling fire. Lancer and Dyson followed them as they moved down the river, away from the glow of the burning cabin and into the paler light of the moon. Lancer looked back once towards Tom's cabin, then turned away. He had seen nothing to arouse his suspicions, and Frank said a silent prayer of thanks for his mother's quick thinking.

'They're gone,' he said, and heard his father draw a deep breath. 'Let's ride down to the cabin.'

The skies had clouded over. A soft rain was falling, and the burning cabin that had been used by young Will Findlay had collapsed in upon itself and was already little more than a pile of glowing, hissing embers.

Inside the other cabin, Beth Shannon had a hot stew in bowls on the table, crisp bread in baskets, coffee bubbling on the stove. They sat down around the table, and the meal was eaten with enjoyment but very little talk. Tom seemed to have withdrawn again. Beth frowned and shook her head at Frank when he looked questioningly at her, and he shrugged and waited for the right moment.

That moment came, inevitably, when they had finished eating and were settled in the battered old easy chairs gathered around the stove, their feet on the soft skins covering the dirt floor. Tom was puffing on his stained, corn cob pipe. His eyes were closed. Beth was clearing the dishes from the table.

'I've been in Mack Findlay's office a couple of times now, talking about this and that,' Frank said. 'He has some theories about Slash S.'

'Slash S went more than a year ago,' Beth said, rattling dishes. 'If that old fool's got theories, he's taken his time voicing them.'

'How much has Pa told you about his child-hood?'

'All there is to tell.'

'So you know about John Shannon?'

'Sure I know about John,' Beth said. She came over, wiping her hands on her pinafore, and sat down between the two men. 'I know what he was like, where he went . . . the fact his ma settled down with another man. . . .'

She seemed to stop short there, and again she was watching her son, as she had on his earlier visit. Did she have her own firm ideas about the loss of Slash S? Mention of John Shannon had not taken her by surprise. Perhaps she was awaiting confirmation of secret thoughts she had been afraid to put into words while she was alone with her ailing husband. Perhaps Frank's presence had not only put the spark of life back into his father's eyes, but also given his mother fresh hope.

'You know that man's name?'

'Nope.'

'Mack seems to think Pa would only have given up Slash S,' Frank said, 'if the rightful heir had come along.'

'His brother?' She frowned, but her eyes seemed guarded. 'What makes him believe Jack Bamber's that man?'

'He's surmising. With some confidence, because how else could Bamber have forced Pa's hand?'

106

'I can think of a number of ways,' Beth Shannon said; 'by threatening me; by suggesting he knew your whereabouts, could hunt you down, have you shot.'

'Pa wouldn't fall for it.'

'Your pa was sick. Still is.' She reached out, took the corn cob pipe from Tom's fingers, placed it on the floor by the stove. He was asleep, slumped in the chair, his breathing deep but uneven. His brow was furrowed, as if he was troubled by dreams.

Beth came silently from her chair, nodded to Frank and he followed her outside. The rain had ceased, the night chill had descended. The horses had been moved out of danger when Will's cabin was torched, and at the eastern end of the gallery they were enveloped in waves of heat billowing across the empty corral from the cabin's glowing embers. There were two chairs. Beth sat down in one. Frank took the rocking chair, aware that this was his father's and that alongside it there was a jug of corn whiskey. In that quiet corner of the wide gallery their faces reflected pale moonlight, and the ruddy glow of the dying fire.

'Everything Mack Findlay told me,' Frank said, 'is guesswork. Like you, he knows the story of my pa's childhood. But the idea that Jack Bamber is Pa's brother is pure conjecture.'

'Then a couple of old-timers have got like

107

minds,' Beth said, and she looked sideways at Frank with a wan smile. 'All right, it's time for me to come clean. I do believe Jack Bamber is John Shannon. Has to be. He turned up out of the blue, and your pa buckled. Just the way he buckled when he was a kid.'

'Why now?'

'Hm?'

'Bamber came after Slash S a year ago, you said. Why not twenty years ago? Or ten? John Shannon is Jesse Shannon's son. He was born on Slash S. What kept him away for all those years, but brought him back now?'

'Hard times?' Beth shrugged. 'Maybe the knowledge that his kid brother had the lot, that he'd turned his back on his inheritance. Could have been eating away at him for a long, long time, and then old age began creeping up on him. . . .'

'What about Pa? Have you put this to him? Have you asked him if he handed the spread over to Bamber because the man's his brother?'

'Asked him, yes, time and time again, but all I get's a blank look, then something about his head doesn't feel too good. Anything to avoid answering.'

'Well, one thing's certain: if you and Mack Findlay are right, then there's no going back, no possible return to Slash S – is there?'

'I believe John Shannon came back home to

claim his inheritance,' Beth said. 'If that's what happened, there's not a damn thing we can do about it.'

Frank sighed.

They sat in silence.

Ember settled in the dying fire with a faint crackle. Sparks drifted across the grass like fireflies. With their sudden wild scattering it was as if Frank Shannon's thoughts had been set free, and suddenly out of nowhere he found himself wondering about the legality of the Slash S takeover *even if Jack Bamber really was John Shannon and the rightful heir.* Could a man show up out of the blue, thirty years after the death of his father, and snatch an inheritance away from the brother who has dedicated his life to maintaining the property? Wasn't there something, anything, that could legally prevent that happening? Something, perhaps, to do with possession becoming legal ownership after a certain time has passed? Were there no safeguards in place to protect the vulnerable against an eventuality such as this sudden takeover?

As if sensing the turmoil in her son's mind, Beth Shannon's words cut through Frank's thoughts, so softly that he only just heard them.

'In the end,' she said, 'despite what I believe and what Mack Findlay's told you *he* believes – it's all surmise.' She turned her head to look levelly at Frank. 'We've got to do something, take this thing further, haven't we? – because I'd hate to think an old man's rotting away in a woodland shack just because nobody would rouse themselves enough to get to the truth.'

THIRTEEN

Frank Shannon's business next day was in Shannon Plains. Since getting out of jail he'd talked to his pa, with no luck. His ma had told him what she believed, and Mack Findlay had finally spilled the beans, but, like Beth Shannon's, his theories were based on guesswork. Now it was time to talk to the law.

Someone, somewhere, was jealously guarding the truth. If Eli Simm was not that man. . . .

Shannon rode in early, his horse one of the first to disturb the dust of Main Street, his arrival acknowledged by a casual wave from George Young who watched with interest from his livery barn as Shannon cut across the street and tied up in front of the jail.

Shannon appreciated the irony of what he was doing. Not many men assault a deputy when breaking out of jail then call back in for a cosy chat with the marshal. And, leaning nonchalantly in the doorway of the jail, Eli Simm was biting back a smile as his one good eye observed Shannon's approach.

The office was empty. No sign of Ed Baines. Maybe he was out back passing breakfast to Will Findlay. But not on a tin tray!

Shannon grinned.

Behind the desk, Simm cocked his head questioningly.

'I was thinking, Ed Baines being somewhere else allows us to get on with serious talking,' Shannon said, and he dragged up a chair and sat down. 'Mostly about the men you lock up for rustling without first checking the facts.'

'When Lancer and Dyson brought you in,' Simm said, 'you didn't look too much like a man returning home to the take over the running of the family spread. Jack Bamber's been losing cattle. You were caught with one of his cows and a hot branding iron.' He lifted his shoulders, spread his hands. 'Then people in town came forward, said they recognized you – vouched for you. . . .'

'That's me sorted out – but what about Will Findlay?'

'Ed rode on up Sweetwater Creek when I was talking to your ma. He found those cattle without too much trouble. Will admitted he'd took them.'

'What Will did,' Frank Shannon said, 'was take cattle from a man who doesn't own them, and return them to the man who does.'

'Ah.' Simm nodded slowly. 'So now we get down to the real point of this early morning visit.'

'That we do,' Shannon said. He hesitated, watched the lean and enigmatic marshal lean back in his chair and light a cigarette, realized that this man could be in Jack Bamber's pocket and, if so, there was danger ahead if Shannon said too much. But he also remembered his first sight of this man, the marshal's flush of anger at Deek Lancer's insolence, the intelligence shining in that one good eye.

'I'd guess that Jack Bamber pays your wages,' Shannon said, 'but despite that you remain very much your own man.'

The comment sank like a stone. Simm inhaled some cigarette smoke, sat and waited.

Again Shannon smiled. 'That leads me to believe that if I discover there's something about Bamber's takeover of Slash S stinks like a dead coyote – you'll keep an open mind.'

'If you've finished discussing me,' Simm said, 'maybe we can talk about you. As the heir to Slash S, you're naturally riled that someone's pulled the rug out from under a nice settled future. But settin' that understandable bitterness to one side – what makes you believe there was something wrong with the takeover?'

'Bamber brought in an out-of-town lawyer. Broke into Mack Findlay's office to get the deeds.

Got them witnessed by Billy Bedford – then sacked him.'

'Those actions can look black or white,' Simm said, 'dependin' on which side of the fence you're sittin'. A man's entitled to bring his own lawyer. Mack Findlay was out of town, the office keys in his pocket, and Bamber was in a hurry. Bedford was due to retire – hell, you could've been away twice seven years and still work that out.'

'And?'

Simm frowned at his cigarette, looked up. 'And what?'

'And my pa was there, signed on the bottom line – so everything was legal and above-board?'

'Yep, I'd say Tom Shannon bein' present clinches the deal,' Simm said. He smiled crookedly. 'Only I guess you're now going to prove me wrong.'

Shannon shook his head. 'Not yet. But I am going to look into it. I came here first to let you know what's happening, and to find out where you stand.'

'On the side of the law,' Simm said without hesitation. 'Jack Bamber didn't pin this badge on my vest. The town council elected me before he got his foot in the door – and after that there was nothing he could do.'

'From his manner, Lancer sees you in a different light.'

'Like his and Bamber's pet lawman?' And now

114

Simm grinned openly. 'I humour men of that type. They lead shallow lives, I let a little sun shine in.'

Shannon nodded. 'Good. Because I've talked to just about everyone likely to know anything, and there's only one place left to go. Slash S was taken away from Tom Shannon, so I'd say that's where the truth lies.'

Bamber wrapped up Slash S with the help of a lawyer, Shannon remembered as he left the jail. Two could play at that game. What was done by Bamber on that day twelve months ago was probably beyond his power to change, but the slim chance he had would surely be given some weight if there was a sharp legal mind listening to any arguments. And maybe, by his presence, preventing violence.

Accordingly, Shannon's next stop after the jail was again at the offices of former lawyer Mack Findlay. Findlay, he knew, was tied up trying to extract his only son from the clutches of the law. But he was also suffering from intense feelings of guilt brought on by Shannon's return. So maybe a visit to Bamber would be killing two birds with the one stone. If the man from the Big Bend country could be sent packing, Tom Shannon would be back with Slash S, and the law would be forced to drop the charges against Will Findlay.

Mack Findlay was willing to try, but not optimistic.

'Talking to Bamber,' he said over his shoulder, as they left his office and walked in opposite directions to collect their horses, 'is like talking to a skinned pole that's been propped up in the sun and left to dry out. His ego's so big a man would need an axe to cut him down to size.'

They rode into the Slash S to a silence that seemed strangely ominous. The yard was empty. No smoke issued from the bunkhouse chimney. The house looked deserted. A lone, sway-backed horse dozed in the corral.

'I told you Bamber was cutting down,' Findlay said thoughtfully, a diminutive but confident figure in the saddle as he reined in and looked about him. Under his skinny right leg a heavy shotgun jutted from a leather boot. His eyes were not that good, he'd told Shannon, 'But with that beauty spraying lead shot a yard wide I can hit a fly at twenty paces.'

Shannon was also puzzled by the lack of activity. 'Lancer and Dyson brought in an extra fifty head,' Shannon said. 'I think he's out there with those two, and Owen and Draper. He'll be doing some fast branding.'

'Which leaves us,' Findlay said, 'with the place to ourselves.'

Shannon looked at him. 'Mack, are you

116

suggesting what I think you're suggesting?'

Findlay's look was innocent. 'Me? I'm going to wander over to that handy ridge under the trees, sit down in the sun, rest my weary bones and look at the scenery.'

'Yeah,' Shannon said, swinging out of the saddle. 'And you've still got your own teeth, so I reckon you can whistle if the need should arise.'

'Like a bird,' the old lawyer said, grinning at Shannon as he wheeled his horse and rode back up the slope.

Shannon left his horse ground-hitched, took a final glance around the yard and buildings and ran up the steps onto the house's gallery. The front door was not locked. He opened it and stepped inside. His first time in his old home for a long seven years. A rush of emotion almost took his breath away.

He had expected to find big changes, but as he wandered slowly across the big room he saw few signs of a stranger's presence. There was the same dark timber furniture he had known all his life, the same big, comfortable chairs – and his father's wide desk in its familiar place against the back wall.

If Bamber had incriminating papers, that's where they would be, those – or papers proving the man's absolute right to the Slash S.

With an effort, Shannon pushed those gloomy thoughts into the background. Always listening for the faint rattle of approaching hooves, or for the shrill of Mack Findlay's warning whistle, he crossed to the desk.

On its top the expected clutter. Papers, bills. An oil lamp with smoke-blackened glass chimney. A stained ink bottle, a pen with a twisted nib. Matches, a box of cigars.

And a small, faded tin-type in a rough wooden frame.

With a sick feeling in his stomach, Shannon picked it up.

He was looking at two young men in overalls standing outside the house. One shorter and stockier than the slim boy standing next to him. They were fifteen or sixteen years old. One was clearly Tom Shannon. The other. . . .

'John Shannon,' Shannon said softly. 'Has to be.'

He'd never seen the picture. He was pretty certain it was not his father's. If he was right, then this was one piece of evidence that seemed to be turning conjecture into fact. A picture, telling him a story he didn't want to hear. He was after the truth – but not this.

Hurriedly he shot a glance towards the window, for a moment listened intently to the heavy silence then slid open desk drawers and rummaged through the contents. More papers, bills yellowing with age, cattle roundup figures from years gone by; letters, some with his father's handwriting, others addressed to him; a pretty notebook that had to belong to his mother, Beth.

Frank Shannon's jaw tightened with anger. He took the notebook, slipped it into his pocket. Then he straightened, stared into space and thought hard. What had he got that proved Jack Bamber was really John Shannon? There was the old tin-type – but that was inconclusive. It was pretty clear that the boy with Tom Shannon was his brother John. But did Bamber bring the picture with him from the Big Bend? Or had it been with Tom and Beth ever since they married, hidden away in the drawer because it aroused painful memories?

On its own, it wasn't enough. He needed more, but the longer he stayed in that room, the bigger the risk of Bamber returning. So far there had been no warning from Findlay – but could he rely on the old lawyer?

This time Shannon went to the window and looked out. Squinting into the bright sunlight, he could just see Findlay sitting in the shade beneath the trees on the ridge. Nothing else moved in the empty yard. The only sounds were those of the house timbers creaking in the heat, the plaintive call of a soaring bird, a whicker from the solitary horse answered at once by Shannon's mount which was moving restlessly despite the trailing reins.

Shannon turned away from the window, walked

slowly towards the centre of the room, his eyes trying to take in everything at once. The bright light was glinting on the dark furniture, casting deep shadows in the far corners. There was the desk, a long table, a tall chest of drawers; too much there to search in the time available. The gun cabinet was as he remembered it – but it was empty, and again anger stirred.

And then he saw the pistol.

He'd missed it when he was at the desk, because he'd been too close. It was tucked away in a pigeon hole. All he could see was the muzzle and an inch or so of the barrel – but in the short time he'd been in the room the sun had shifted, and now the blued steel was caught by a shaft of sunlight in which motes danced.

It was a converted Collier pistol, surely the one Mack Findlay had described. Frank Shannon picked it up, hefted the old weapon. He could feel disappointment welling in him, feel his pulse thumping, the uncomfortable tightness in his breathing. He turned the pistol in his hand, looked at the barrel, the cylinder and percussion caps – the rosewood butt, with the initials crudely carved in the shiny wood by a fifteen-year old boy. TS, for Tom Shannon. This must be the pistol John Shannon had coveted, then taken away from his younger brother while his father's laughter rang in his ears.

It was the proof he had been looking for, Frank

Shannon thought bitterly, the evidence he had not wanted to find. There could now be no doubt: Jack Bamber was John Shannon.

And he was still looking with numb dismay at the Collier pistol that had been taken from his father when the front door crashed open.

'This time,' Jack Bamber said, 'you're finished.'

The lean rancher was blocking the doorway. An evil grin split his face. He was obviously jubilant, but Shannon knew he wasn't thinking straight. Triumph at catching Shannon with his pants down had stopped him in his tracks so he could soak up his moment of triumph. But although Shannon's six-gun was in its holster, he was holding a pistol, the old Collier just might be loaded – and Bamber's reaction to what Shannon was about to do would quickly give him the answer.

Frank Shannon snicked back the hammer.

'Stay right where you are,' he said quietly.

Bamber glared in astonishment and stepped forward.

Feeling the prickle of cold sweat, Shannon lifted the pistol, levelled it at Bamber's head. He let the lean man see the white of his knuckle as he put pressure on the trigger. Impressing him with the danger. But was the Collier loaded? Was the mechanism worn by use to a hair trigger. If the answer was a yes to both of those the slightest pressure would be too much and it could all be over. Shannon's scalp prickled at the thought.

Bamber froze, his face pinched and pale with anger. The answer to Shannon's unspoken questions was naked in his eyes: he knew the Collier was loaded and, reluctantly, he stepped back, trying to distance himself from that deadly weapon. Again he was blocking the doorway. Shannon could see Lancer behind him. There was space for the foreman to shoot around his boss. But the risk was too great.

'Make a stupid move,' Shannon said. 'Go on. I'd like nothing better than to plug you between the eyes. But this pistol I'm holding tells a story – doesn't it?'

'Tom Shannon's Collier,' Bamber said.

'Your brother's. His prize possession – the one you took from him.'

'You've done your homework.'

'Thank Mack Findlay for that. He knows Tom well, told me the story—'

As if on cue, the old lawyer's voice rang out from the yard.

'I've got 'em, Frank. Let them inside when they've got rid of their weapons. Do that now, all of you – and anyone trying to pull iron gets cut in half.'

Lancer was looking over his shoulder, apparently watching the lawyer. Then he turned, began unbuckling his gunbelt and gave Bamber a hard push. The rancher stumbled into the room.

There was a succession of thuds as gunbelts were unbuckled and dropped on the board gallery. Lancer walked in, followed by Cole Dyson, blue eyes cold with fury, and the two men Shannon remembered from his first day on Shannon land: Owen and Draper. Those two looked interested, but unconcerned.

Right behind them came Mack Findlay. The big shotgun was levelled and cocked.

Findlay was dangerous, his manner leaving the Slash S men in no doubt that he would pull the trigger if they made a false move, but there was a sheepish look in his eyes when he looked quickly at Shannon. 'They'd passed me before I saw them,' he told Shannon. 'I guess I'm too old for this, must have dozed off. . . .'

'No harm done,' Shannon said. 'I've already told Bamber I've found what I came for, and it's in his favour.'

'What I found,' Bamber said, 'is a drifter inside my house, and would you believe my luck? I've got a lawyer here to prove it.'

'Shannon came looking for evidence to put you in the clear,' Findlay said bluntly. 'How he got it doesn't matter, and if you've got sense you won't push this.' He looked at Shannon. 'You sure that's your pa's pistol?'

'It's got his initials. You told me the story, a converted Collier like this figured in it – so, although I can't be *certain*, I'd say it must be.' He gestured behind him. 'There's also a tin-type there I've not seen before today. Pa and his brother, outside this house.'

'Mine,' Bamber said. 'I took a couple of things with me when I left. That was one of them: you're holding the other – and I'd thank you to point it somewhere else.'

For a long moment there was silence. The other men – Lancer, Dyson, Owen and Lister – had dispersed around the room, either dropping into the big chairs or remaining standing to watch and listen. To Shannon, Lancer seemed to be paying unusually close attention to Bamber's every word. In his turn, Bamber seemed confident, yet wary, as if always conscious of Lancer's attention.

Well, that was as maybe, and something to be mulled over later. For now Frank Shannon knew there was nothing more to say to Bamber, but an awful lot to discuss with Mack Findlay – out of Bamber's earshot.

'I'll take this with me, return it to its owner,' he said to Bamber, and held up the Collier. 'The tin-type's yours to keep.'

He nodded to Findlay. The lawyer made a wide sweep with the cocked shotgun's muzzle, letting each man in turn taste the sharp fear it aroused – then he backed towards the door. There he stood to one side. Shannon slipped through and ran down the steps, swept up the reins and stepped into the saddle. He tucked the Collier into his belt, drew and cocked his Winchester in time to cover Findlay's retreat.

And they were hammering out of the yard in a cloud of dust when, with a swift backward glance, Shannon saw Jack Bamber step out onto the gallery and shade his eyes to watch them leave.

FOURTEEN

'We move now,' Deek Lancer said flatly.

Owen and Draper had been sent back to the bunkhouse. Dyson had been outside to collect their weapons, and was now standing staring broodingly out of the window. Jack Bamber was sitting at the desk, a glass of whiskey in one hand, the old tin-type in the other. He flipped the picture in his fingers then, with a sharp exclamation, tossed it onto the desk where it fell with a clatter.

'It's too soon,' he said.

'That's crazy talk.' Lancer shook his head. 'Shannon and that lawyer won't stop digging. If we don't move fast, it could be too late.'

'I think they're satisfied,' Bamber said. 'I think they came here looking for proof, and went away convinced.' He shook his head. 'Besides, we need horses, a *remuda* – we need more time.'

'Owen and Draper can go get the horses today.

We need thirty. If they go to that feller works his stock in the hills north of here, nobody in town will be any the wiser. Those broncs get used on the drive, then sold along with the cattle.'

'Why is it too soon?' Dyson said, turning away from the window. Still brooding over the indignity they had suffered at the hands of old Mack Findlay, his pale-blue eyes now looked on Bamber with suspicion. 'The herd's ready. *We* can be ready in no time at all. So where's the problem?'

'You two can be ready,' Bamber said. 'I can, at a push – but maybe I've got different ideas.'

Lancer shook his head. 'You're not here to have ideas, Bamber. The only reason you're here at all is because, without you, we couldn't have moved onto Slash S.'

'Maybe now I am here, settled in, I'm getting to like it.'

'Ah.' Lancer looked at Cole Dyson, and winked. 'The old bandido wants to settle down, Cole, put a rocking chair out there on the gallery, end his days lazin' in the sun.'

'Anything wrong with that?' Bamber was looking challengingly at both men.

'What's wrong with it,' Dyson said, 'is we rode all the way from Texas to make ourselves a heap of money. Now, if you want to end your days in peace like Deek says, then I can help you on your way right now. Dump your dead body to rot in the sun. If that doesn't sound too appealing, well, we just do like Deek says: we move now. As soon as we've got the *remuda*, the supplies we need from town, we're ready to roll.'

'The hard bits're done, the job you needed me for is finished,' Bamber said. 'Take the cattle to market, sell them and move on. You don't need me.'

'Yeah,' Deek Lancer said, and now all amusement had drained away and his eyes were hard and cold. 'But that leaves you settin' here on Slash S with a heap of cash in the bank—'

'I'll have the cash, you'll have profits from the sale of all that prime beef.' Bamber smiled thinly. 'Sounds a reasonable split to me.'

'All depends how you do the calculating,' Lancer said. 'The way I see it, we finish the drive, sell that beef then put all the cash in one heap and split three ways. That means cash from the bank, and cash for the sale. I'd hate to see you taking all that bank cash for yourself, me and Cole splitting what cash we get for the cattle – in a competitive market – and ending up losers.'

'Prime beef,' Bamber said. 'You know you'll come out on top.'

'What I know is you're in this to the end,' Lancer said. 'We're in this together. We move that herd out as soon as we're ready, settle up at the end of the drive. After that. . . .' He shrugged.

'That's what bothers me,' Bamber said quietly. 'The bits going unsaid. "After that" you said, and left it unfinished.' He shook his head. 'Well, when the drive's over and there's a heap of money on the table you'll be removing two men from the equation so you, me and Dyson get a bigger share – but I can't help seeing the elimination of two men leading to the obvious conclusion that a two way split's more attractive, and temptation raising its ugly head.'

'Funny you should say that,' Cole Dyson said, 'because the same damn thought had crossed my mind more than once – only in my version it was you using a six-gun to boost your share.'

And the look in his cold blue eyes told Jack Bamber he could plan until the cows came home, and Lancer and Dyson would still be one step ahead of him.

FIFTEEN

'What he said,' Frank Shannon said, 'is that the pistol I was pointing at his head, this pistol' – he placed it on the marshal's desk – 'is Tom Shannon's old Collier.'

Eli Simm nodded. 'So? You found it at Slash S, on your pa's desk. It's got his initials carved in the butt. And it fits the story Mack told you. Doesn't that seem to prove it did belong to Tom when he was a young lad, and if Bamber brought it with him—'

'Yeah, but why would he say it's *Tom Shannon's*. That has a false ring to it. If it was me I'd've said, sure, that pistol's *my brother's* Collier.'

Simm looked at Mack Findlay. 'Did you pick up on that?'

'I thought it was strange.'

'Even from a man who hasn't seen or heard of his brother for . . . what, fifty years or more?'

'Sure.' Findlay nodded. 'Despite that. I think it

was a slip, something he didn't even consider saying differently, and so it'll never strike him that what he said is a dead giveaway.'

Simm sucked his teeth. 'That bad?'

'Bad enough,' Frank Shannon said, 'for me to suggest the man out there is not John Shannon.' He thought for a moment. 'Another thing. The tin-type I saw showed the two brothers side by side. I had no trouble recognizing my pa, but Bamber looks nothing like the older lad.'

'All right,' Simm said, 'if he's not Shannon then who the hell is he?'

Frank Shannon shrugged, but it was a shrug that simply meant he was considering the question. His outlook had changed after the talk with Bamber. Before, he had been despondent; now he was so optimistic he was consciously having to damp down his elation. Something was terribly wrong with the whole Slash S setup, and that could only be good for Tom Shannon. Not only was the ranch doing little more than stagger from one lazy day to the next, but Shannon had suddenly begun to question Bamber's position. There were three men involved in the Slash S takeover. On the face of it, Bamber was John Shannon, and in charge; Lancer was the foreman, Dyson his useful sidekick.

But were they?

Watching those three men in the big ranch house, Shannon had sensed a subtle shift in authority. Of the three, Deek Lancer had impressed as the most dominant personality. And now Shannon was wondering – after raising the possibility that Bamber was not John Shannon – if he had always been playing second fiddle to the big foreman. Maybe Lancer was the brains behind whatever was going on, and he'd needed someone to play the part of John Shannon; some-one he could use, an older man, a man in his sixties. . . .

Those thoughts raced through his mind while Simm watched and waited patiently.

'If he's not John Shannon, we know how he hoodwinked my pa,' Shannon said now. 'He showed him the pistol. He showed him the tin-type; and I'd say he had a load of memories that only a brother could know.'

'How?'

'For the answer to that,' Shannon said, 'you'd need to do some hard searching in the Big Bend country. You'd need,' he said, 'to find out what happened to the real John Shannon.'

In the sudden silence, Mack Finlay pushed out of his chair and wandered through to the cells. He'd spoken briefly to Simm about his son, Will, when he and Shannon rode in from the Slash S. Nothing had changed, Simm told him, the boy would still be charged with rustling – and that was another reason why Frank Shannon was keen to get this mess settled. The circuit judge was due in a couple of days. If, when he arrived in town, Jack Bamber was still owner of the Slash S, things would look bleak for the kid who'd been helping out at Sweetwater Creek.

Simm looked at Shannon, and shook his head ruefully. As he did so they both heard the rattle of a wagon. Shannon twisted in his seat to look out of the window.

It was Lancer and Dyson. Both men jumped down, crossed the sidewalk and entered the general store.

'That reminds me, your pa's in town,' Simm said. 'He and your ma brought the buckboard in early. They usually come in this time of the month to pick up supplies.'

'I'll wander over that way shortly,' Shannon said, 'give them a hand to load up.'

He left his chair and walked to the door. For the first time he noticed his pa's old buckboard outside George Young's place. His ma was standing by it, talking to the deputy, big Ed Baines. Shannon switched his gaze back to the general store; could see, through the open door in the dim interior, Lancer leaning on the counter, Dyson pacing restlessly.

'I wonder what the hell they're up to?' Frank Shannon said.

Simm had walked up behind him. 'Ranchers sell cows. Some time soon Bamber'll drive his to market. Why should that bother you?'

'You've not been listening,' Shannon said, and swung to face the marshal. 'Bamber could be selling cows that don't belong to him.'

'Ah, yes.' Simm's eyes were mild. 'You don't think Bamber is John Shannon – yet your pa gave him Slash S. You've suggested the truth may lie somewhere in the the Big Bend country – and we know how distant that is. Well, if you come up with proof, I'll talk to Bamber. Until that happens, I've got a prisoner and his lawyer to talk to and premises to get ready for a trial.'

'Tell Mack Findlay I'll see him later,' Shannon said tightly, and walked out of the office.

Anger stayed with Shannon as he cut across the street to the livery barn, yet deep down he knew Simm was right. Shannon needed proof, and he had the feeling that time was running out; sensed that Jack Bamber – or the men who were using him – would very soon strip Slash S clean and turn it into a ghost ranch. If Shannon tackled Bamber again, he'd learn nothing. And, unless there had been some remarkable changes, for reasons known only to himself his pa was likely to remain close mouthed.

So what now?

The Big Bend was the country bordering the deep swing of the Rio Grande, Mexico's north-western border. Riding there was out of the question. But what about the telegraph? That,

Shannon thought, was a possibility – and as a lawman Simm would know where to send the message, maybe even who to ask.

Anger was swiftly swamped by renewed urgency. He hesitated, paused in the dust and looked back towards the jail, then continued on to where his mother was still talking to Baines.

The big deputy saw him coming. Beth Shannon touched his arm, her eyes were twinkling.

'Ed was telling me the terrible things you did to him,' she said. 'I think you owe him an apology.'

'I'll give him one willingly,' Shannon said, 'if he'll do something for me in return.'

'Mistakes were made, on both sides,' Baines said. His eyes were hard, but not unfriendly. He stuck out his hand, and as Shannon grasped it he said, 'You're a pain in the neck' – he winked at Beth Shannon – 'but you shouldn't have been in jail so I guess I owe you one favour.'

'I'd like you to ask your boss,' Shannon said, 'to telegraph someone, anyone, down in the Big Bend country of Texas. He'll do it. He knows I need information about a man called John Shannon.'

Beth frowned. 'Won't work,' she said. 'John changed his name.'

Frank Shannon shook his head. 'Not first off, not when he was very young. When he moved down there with my grandma they were on their own. He would have lived for some time under his own name.'

'If I've got the age right, then you're going back an awful long way,' Baines said.

'It's likely to be a small, sleepy town, and people who live in those places have long memories,' Shannon said.

'A long shot,' said Baines.

'It's all I've got,' Shannon said.

Baines spread his hands, then nodded agreement. As he turned and walked away towards the jail, Shannon looked at Beth.

'Where's Pa?'

'Inside, talking to George.'

'Has he said anything?'

'I've not asked.'

'Maybe George has got him talking,' Shannon said, and he led the way slowly into the barn.

The livery-barn owner with the tanned and shaven head was leaning against a stall talking to Tom Shannon. That in itself was promising, Frank Shannon thought. Was his pa coming out of it? Had his son's arrival and the recent happenings at Sweetwater Creek snapped him out of whatever had been ailing him?

'I've not asked,' Beth said softly behind him, 'but something's changed, he's different now. . . .'

'Slash S is in town,' Frank said, making the remark casually to George Young but for Tom Shannon's benefit. 'I think they're planning a drive to market.'

'Too soon,' Tom Shannon said bluntly. 'But they'll make money anyhow. . . .' He looked at Beth. 'Money that's rightfully ours.'

'But if Bamber's your brother,' Frank Shannon said, feigning puzzlement to draw his father out, 'and he's the rightful heir. . . .'

'If. . . .' Tom Shannon said, and he looked apologetically at Beth. 'I've thought long and hard. A lot of the time I've been someplace else, a befuddled old fool wallowing in misery – but in the times when my mind's been clear I've been thinking more and more how it might be possible for a clever man to get the right information to fool an old codger.'

Frank Shannon felt an enormous flood of relief.

'Ed Baines is talking to Simm now,' he said. 'If Bamber is an imposter, he got that information from somewhere. If we can find where, and prove it—'

'He's already took my cash,' Tom Shannon said, and he shook his head as Beth moved close enough to grasp his hand tightly.

'Trouble is,' George Young said, 'until you get that proof, Frank, you go after that herd and you'll end up in the next cell to Will Findlay.'

'I'm going to talk to Mack now. He's been in this with me. There must be some other way of getting to Bamber. News from the Big Bend would settle it, but I'd like to figure out some way of doing it without wasting all that time.'

'If they move that herd out now,' George said, 'you'll be following a long trail.'

'Nah.' Shannon found himself grinning. 'A trail drive moves real slow. Even old Mack Findlay should come up with something before it's gone too far.'

SIXTEEN

Frank Shannon spent the next hour down at the general store helping his father load the buckboard with provisions. And once again he encountered a strange face doing a familiar job. Bill Todd was the new owner. Cheerful but taciturn, he nevertheless disclosed that Deek Lancer of Slash S had loaded provisions for the second time in a couple of days, and had informed Todd that as soon as they had their *remuda* they'd be hitting the trail.

After that news, Shannon worked on with his mind elsewhere. Finally, when the wagon was almost ready to pull out, he made his excuses, kissed Beth, handed her the pretty notebook he'd found and grinned at her surprise, then left her and hurried across the street.

'It'll all work out,' he said as he left his mother. 'I'll make sure of that.'

But could he be sure?

He was after the truth, and the truth in the shape of Jack Bamber was preparing to hit the trail. If Bamber had his remuda, each hour that passed would put him further away from Shannon Plains. And if he got the herd to market before news came through from the Big Bend – which could take days – the Shannons could forget about Slash S, at least in terms of a working ranch. The capital was in the bank, in Bamber's name. He would withdraw that cash, pool it with the proceeds from the cattle sale – and disappear.

So, yes, they had to get at the truth, and quickly.

Feeling bleak, Shannon went into the jail office. Old Mack Findlay had come through from his talk with Will and was standing looking out of the window. Simm was at the desk fiddling with papers, but his mind was clearly not on the job.

'Closest I could get,' he said, 'was a friend of mine down near the Mex border. I telegraphed him, he came straight back, told me he'll sniff around.'

Shannon nodded his thanks and dropped heavily into a chair. He looked at Findlay's back.

'How's Will?'

'Stoic.' The lawyer turned. 'We're all hanging like crazy on the word of a man we've never met, lives way on the far side of Texas.'

'I'd be mighty surprised if Frank Shannon ain't passed through that region on his travels,' the

140

marshal said. He sent his pen clattering onto the desk and sat back. When he rubbed his blank white eye, it creaked curiously.

Shannon couldn't help grinning. 'Yeah, life sure is strange. I crossed the Mex border at Ojinaga, spent a week down there before taking a long sweep up through the Cimarrons. Who's to say I didn't talk to the man once called himself John Shannon—'

'If he's alive.'

That was Simm, and he caught their attention.

'That's the answer,' Shannon said. 'I think you've hit on it: John Shannon *must* be dead.'

'Bamber's got things belong to him,' Simm said. He poked the Collier pistol, still lying on the desk. 'I suspect an old man wouldn't give this away in a hurry.'

'Or a precious tin-type,' Shannon said. 'Not if he thought anything of his brother.'

'According to the story, he didn't, when he was a boy,' Mack Findlay said, coming away from the window and dragging up a chair. 'But that's always bothered me. Age changes men. We mellow. After all those years I can't see John Shannon doing what he's supposed to have done: taken Slash S away from his brother, Tom Shannon, and left him with nothing.'

Simm shook his head. 'Old-timers. They'd come to an arrangement. Run the spread together. Retire and sit in the sun, let their young

141

kinfolk do the hard work.'

Shannon grunted. 'Maybe if I'd come home sooner. . . .'

'Or maybe if Bamber had a son he'd brought with him who could run the ship in your absence,' Findlay said. 'Only now we're talking nonsense. That didn't happen, because we all know this Bamber is *not* John Shannon – but we've got no proof. So we're sitting waiting to hear from a stranger who's got no reason to hurry, the circuit judge'll be here in less than forty-eight hours and I've got no defence for my own son—'

'And the man who stole everything from my father is preparing to cut and run,' Frank Shannon said.

Eli Simm sighed, and reached for the makings. 'Sometimes the law don't help,' he said. 'We've worked our way around so we've got a pretty fair idea of the wrongs that have been done – but my hands are tied.'

There seemed to be nothing anyone could do or say.

It was perhaps natural that Frank Shannon and Mack Findlay should find themselves that early evening at a table in the almost empty bar of what Shannon called the Sunrise saloon.

'Or Sunset,' Findlay said, looking sideways at him.

Frank nodded. 'Yeah, I'd forgotten that – or maybe I've just been looking at it from one side.'

'Sunrise one side of the sign, Sunset the other,' Findlay said. 'Works fine if you come through town the same way every day. Otherwise. . . .' He shrugged, poured a fresh drink, stared into his glass.

'Whichever way you look at it right now,' Shannon said, 'the sun's gone down and there's still no news.'

'You seen the size of Texas?'

'Ridden across it, all four directions.'

'Then you know we'll likely be standing here this time next year and Tom and your ma will still be out there on Sweetwater Creek. My boy Will. . . .'

'Hey,' Shannon said quietly, 'I've been fighting misery for more than a year, it did me no good—'

'Here comes Simm.'

Shannon grunted in surprise. Just when you least expect something. . . .

The marshal stomped over, sat down, swept off his hat and leaned back.

'Fort Davis came through.'

Shannon frowned. 'Where?'

'Fort Davis, Texas. Feller I know's a lawman there.' He was looking at Shannon. 'I told you, down near the Mex border.'

'Yeah, yeah.' Shannon nodded quickly. 'So what's he come up with?'

143

'John Shannon was well known—'

'Was?'

'Hold on, I'm gettin' to it.' Simm reached for the bottle, took a long pull, put it down again with a sigh. 'Yeah, like I was saying, he was known, he had a reputation. First as John Shannon. Later as Tex Long. Took the second name from his stepfather – although there was never any record of a marriage. . . .'

Mack Findlay was nodding as the story unfolded. Shannon was waiting, his fists planted on the table either side of his glass. He knew with a sick foreboding exactly what was coming, and his tension must have been communicated to Simm because the lawman was frowning as he continued.

'He took the Tex moniker, I guess because he moved there from Kansas, but also because it had a good ring – considering the kind of work he was doing.'

'Wrangler?' Mack Findlay said, hazarding a guess.

'Bank robber,' Eli Simm said – and stopped short as Frank Shannon put his face in his hands.

'Jesus Christ!' Shannon said. He pulled his hands away, looked at Simm. 'Died a year ago – right? Shot outside the bank in Fort Davis?'

'That's exactly what happened,' Simm said.

'Where does Bamber come into it?'

'They always worked together. He was

mounted, holding Long's horse—'

'I didn't see him,' Shannon said.

If he was shocked, confused, Simm hid it well. 'Oh, he was there, and he lit out when a stranger collided with Long outside the bank and was fast enough to gun him down – but not before Long had let loose with his shotgun and killed a young woman.'

'That was a long telegraph message,' Findlay said, watching Shannon.

'It'll do as proof that Bamber's taken over Slash S under false pretences,' Simm said. 'We've got what we need, which should leave Tom Shannon feeling pretty good.'

Frank Shannon's smile was bitter. 'Oh, sure, he'll feel real good – until he finds out his son pulled a six-gun and shot his brother down like a dog.'

'You were in the wrong place,' Mack Findlay said. 'From this point of view. In the eyes of the lawman down in Fort Davis, you were in the right place and did a fine job.'

'If I'd been someplace else,' Shannon said, 'the bank robbers would have got away, that young woman would be alive, my pa would still be running Slash S.'

'You don't know that,' Findlay said. 'The bank robbery could have been their last fling before riding north for juicier pickings.'

'That's right,' Eli Simm said. 'John Shannon died, so Bamber decided to work this on his own. That makes it illegal. If John Shannon himself had come to take over Slash S, the spread would've been lost to your pa for all time.'

'Are you saying that by killing his brother, I did Pa a good turn?'

'John Shannon was born bad, or grew up bad,' Simm said. 'Either way, your pa hasn't seen him since they were young boys. If he knew the truth, would he be any happier?'

'What he doesn't know can't hurt him,' Mack Findlay said.

'Oh no.' Shannon shook his head, appalled by what they were suggesting. He slopped whiskey into his glass, stared at it, then pushed it away. 'No, he has to be told, I can't—'

'Tell him the one fact he needs to know: John Shannon died in Fort Davis,' Findlay said.

'I shot him—'

'Your pa's an old man with memories,' Findlay said. 'Why ruin the time he's got left?'

'Because I set out to discover the truth,' Shannon said. 'That means the whole truth. I can't be selective. At the outset I didn't know the part I'd played. But not knowing then doesn't excuse not telling now—'

'We're wasting time,' Eli Simm cut in.

'Time *and* breath, when there's a night's work ahead of us,' Mack Findlay said. 'Two things need doing in a hurry. We get my boy out of jail, and we have a long talk with Jack Bamber.'

Simm grunted, and shook his head. 'Easy now, Mack. Sure, everything points to Bamber bein' a crook; everything points to him riding north with the intention of impersonating another man so he could illegally take possession of property. However—'

'Yes, all right.' Findlay, the lawyer, was already ahead of the marshal, and reluctantly nodded agreement. 'Nothing's settled until the last loose end's tied. The telegraph you've got your hands on is just another bit of paper. Only one man can give us the truth. Face to face.'

'And your boy'll come to no harm spending one more night in jail.'

Findlay pursed his lips. 'One more night – if we catch up with Bamber.'

'We'll catch him,' Frank Shannon said. 'They'll've moved the herd, but not all that far before bedding down for the night. And they won't move again until dawn. Gives us time to get some sleep before riding out and catching them with their pants down.' He grinned. 'A man,' he said, 'is always at his worst when he's half awake with his legs tangled in dew-soaked blankets.'

SEVENTEEN

It was quickly decided that hammering down on the sleeping herd with a posse of armed men would inevitably lead to a bloodbath. And, once again, Shannon could see no better way of approaching Bamber than with Mack Findlay at his side. Between them they would be armed with force, wisdom and the authority of a respected lawyer which – Shannon fervently hoped – would again cause the Bamber crew to think twice before using gunplay.

Eli Simm objected. He told them that if the story wired to him was true and Bamber had been John Shannon's partner in crime, nothing Shannon or Findlay could say would divert him from his course. But it was Simm who had urged caution, he who had suggested that, despite the news from the Big Bend, only Bamber himself could tell them the truth. So, reluctantly, he went along with the idea of Shannon and Findlay confronting Bamber – but with an unshakeable proviso: Ed Baines would stay in town, Simm would ride with Shannon and Findlay, drop back when they approached the herd but remain close enough to move in fast at the first sign of trouble.

He imposed that condition, and refused to budge.

It was midnight when they retired for the night. Simm went home, Mack Findlay slept on the cot in his office, Frank Shannon bedded down in the cell next to a grinning Will Findlay. This time his door was unlocked. And, before going to sleep, he took his supper in the jail office with a friendly Ed Baines.

It was Baines who woke him at four o'clock. After a quick swill in cold water, Shannon crossed the street, roused Mack Findlay, and together they rode to Simm's house on the outskirts of town. From there, in the cold half light an hour before dawn, the three men headed out for the Slash S.

The detour was necessary. If the herd was on the move, it would be heading west. But all they had to go on was the knowledge that Lancer and Dyson had been in town loading up with provisions. They needed to know for sure that Bamber had started the drive, and moved out.

That took them half an hour. Slash S was deserted, house, bunkhouse and corral all empty.

'Now we move fast,' Frank Shannon said, and

they turned their mounts so that the lightening skies were at their backs, and lit out across country.

They followed the broad trail beaten by the Slash S herd, tasting the dust that had never entirely settled, Shannon knowing well that he had been right: Bamber had been impatient to start the drive, content to cover just a few miles before bedding the herd down for the night.

In fact it was no more than ten miles. Shortly after fording a wide, fast-running creek they saw a thin pencil of smoke from a fire, the low mist like a blanket close to the ground and knew that, in the chill air, it was condensation from the mass of warm bodies. Then they heard the sounds. The animals were on their feet and restless. They were thirsty. Their soft lowing carried on the still air.

'A small herd, but fine stock,' Simm said. 'That smoke pinpoints the camp-fire – and there's a stand of trees between us and them.'

Shannon nodded. 'We'll go straight on in, catch 'em when they're bent over their pork and beans.'

'That won't put them in the mood for fightin'.' The marshal's mind was still on tactics. 'See where those trees cloak a rise to the north?' he said. 'That's where I'll be. If there's trouble, I can pick off every damn one of them with a rifle.'

'If there is trouble,' Shannon said, 'it'll be over before you can blink.'

'Yeah, but watch Lancer and Dyson, don't let them get behind you,' Simm said, preparing to move away. 'I've been doing some thinking, and I've got me a sneaking suspicion that feller's being used.'

As he rode off, Shannon caught Findlay nodding.

'You agree with him?'

'I'm pretty sure you do, too. You were watching Lancer at Slash S, you saw what I saw: he had his eye on Bamber, sort of making sure the old feller said the right thing, let nothing slip. . . .'

They had been riding while talking. Now they were drawing close to the growth of stunted trees where the Slash S men had made camp and lit their fire. Close by there was a temporary rope corral for the remuda. Two men could be seen out riding on the flanks of the restless herd. The other three – Bamber, Lancer and Dyson – were breaking camp and had not yet noticed the approaching riders.

But that couldn't last. Shannon and Findlay were fifty yards away when Lancer heard them. He spun, stabbed a hand to his holster. Metal glinted as he drew his six-gun.

He was grinning as they approached. 'Why am I not surprised?'

'Maybe you're intelligent enough to realize

151

Frank Shannon's return spelled the end of the good life.'

That was Findlay. They drew rein as he spoke. Dyson had backed away from the fire. Shannon noticed his horse was saddled, saw the rifle he favoured jutting from its leather boot. Bamber had been using the side of his foot to rake earth over the fire's hot embers. In the morning light that seemed to bleach flesh from bones his grey hair was thin and he looked old and tired.

Lancer was shaking his head. 'I'm smart enough to know an old man and a drunk with their minds fogged with crazy notions can't ride up and stop a legitimate cattle drive.'

'Two men,' Cole Dyson said, 'cain't do nothing except turn around and get the hell out of here,' and in one fluid motion he stepped up to his horse and slid the Winchester from its boot.

'Which is it, Bamber?' Shannon said. 'Are you a rancher taking his herd to market, or a thief about to sell another man's cattle?'

'Why don't you call him by his real name?' Lancer said.

'I'm John Shannon,' Bamber said. 'This is my herd.'

'No.' Shannon shook his head. 'John Shannon died outside a bank in Fort Davis, Texas. You were there.'

'You're crazy, *I'm* Shannon—'

'Look at me,' Frank Shannon said. 'Then turn

your mind back to when John Shannon stepped out of that bank carrying a gunny-sack, and walked into a fast-shooting stranger—'

'Jesus Christ!' Bamber said. He took a step backwards. His face went white.

'What's he talking about?' Lancer said.

'It's him. He shot John Shannon,' Bamber said. 'I—'

His words were choked off by the crack of Dyson's rifle. The bullet slammed into his back. He fell forward, sprawling face down across the remains of the fire. His shirt began to smoulder.

Shannon was helpless. He was pinned by the grinning Lancer's six-gun, and now he realized Dyson had seen movement in the woods when he turned to draw his Winchester. He watched in horror as the blue-eyed gunman stepped back to his horse. He flipped the Winchester across the saddle and snapped three fast shots towards the stand of timber. There was a sudden flurry of movement. They all saw the flash of a white face, heard the distant crackle of undergrowth as a heavy body fell.

'Two ways we can do this,' Lancer said. 'You turn around and ride away. Or we plug you and dump you in the woods with your pard – who is it? Simm?' He didn't wait for an answer, but went on, 'Either way, me and Cole are pushing on with the herd. A day's ride, no more, and we're done. So back off, forget this happened. That way, Tom

Shannon'll get his spread back. Any other way, and there'll be more blood spilled.'

The sharp crack of the Winchester had disturbed the herd. The restless lowing had become nervous bellowing. Dust rose as steers began stamping and snorting. Heads were tossing. Long horns flashed white in the brightening sunlight.

The two outriders were looking towards the campsite. One shouted something. And suddenly Shannon realized Mack Findlay was no longer by the fire. He had used the few seconds of explosive action to fade away – and nobody had noticed him leave. Lancer and Dyson were looking at Shannon, waiting for his next move. Shannon was returning their stares, but beyond them he could see the old lawyer riding past the nervous herd and approaching the two distant riders.

'It's ten miles back to town,' Shannon said. 'A twenty-mile round trip. I'll be back in three hours with Ed Baines and a posse. That herd's got one pace, it'll hold you back. You're finished, Lancer.'

Lancer laughed. 'You don't leave me much choice.'

His meaning was clear. He let his eyes go blank. Shannon saw his finger begin to tighten on the trigger.

Then Mack Findlay's shotgun blasted.

Lancer's eyes widened with shock. He spun. As he did so Findlay's second barrel roared. It was

joined by the rapid snapping of the two riders'
six-guns – and suddenly the herd was on the
move.

Findlay had chosen well. Two miles back they
had crossed a fast-flowing creek. The herd could
smell the water. And Findlay had ridden around
the nervous cattle and used the powerful roar of
his shotgun to set them moving in the direction
they already wanted to go.

Lancer cursed. The herd was still a hundred
yards away. He seemed to be caught between
settling the business with Shannon, and running
for his horse. In the end he did nothing. As he
teetered, going neither one way nor the other,
Shannon drew his six-gun and shot him in the
chest. Shock registered on the big foreman's face.
His pistol fell from his fingers. Then he back
pedalled, and sat down heavily. Blood trickled
from his open mouth. His eyes were already glaz-
ing.

Also caught by indecision, Cole Dyson had
been watching the herd, listening to the growing
thunder of hooves. At the crack of Shannon's
pistol, he sprang into life. He was already close to
his horse. Now he dived full length, wriggled
under the horse's belly and came up on the other
side. Still clutching his Winchester.

Shannon flashed a look at the running steers.
Fifty yards. They were moving, but not yet at a
dead run. And, like the men, they were faced with

decisions. Findlay's shotgun had roared behind them. Now they were listening to more gunfire – but from their front.

And then Dyson's Winchester cracked and spat fire.

Shannon felt the wind of the slug and knew that only Dyson's growing panic had ruined his aim. The rifle cracked again as he dropped to the ground. The slug hissed across Shannon's head. Behind the spooked horse Dyson was hopping about, never still. All Shannon could see of him were his legs. He snapped a shot, saw dust spurt between the gunman's boots.

Then, over the pounding of hooves, a distant rifle cracked. Eli Simm, back on his feet on the edge of the woods. Dyson stopped moving. Shannon saw the legs stiffen. Then they buckled. As his horse whinnied, reared, and raced away, Dyson hit the ground like an empty sack.

And now the herd, at full gallop, was thirty yards away.

In the split second he had left, Shannon reacted instinctively. He turned to face the onrushing steers. Out of the billowing dust and the pounding madness he picked the biggest target he could find. Fanning the hammer, he emptied his six-gun. As if in a slow-motion dream he saw each bullet drill into the skull of his chosen animal. Eyes rolling white the steer continued to thunder towards him, drew perilously close – then in the space of a single stride collapsed in a heap. It thumped down close enough for Shannon to be splashed by its blood, to feel its hot, dying breath. When it hit the ground, Shannon went down with it. He rolled, flattened himself to the ground and tucked himself hard against the warm bulk of the dead steer.

And the racing herd parted, and went around the obstacle. Thunder was in Shannon's ears. His eyes were squeezed shut. His mouth and nose were clogged with dust. Beneath him, the ground trembled. For an instant, with a twinge of pity, he thought of Lancer, Dyson, and Jack Bamber, lying unprotected in the path of the stampeding herd. Then he hardened his heart. Those men had done wrong. Now they were dead. He lay still, listened as the drum of hooves began to fade; opened his eyes to see the tail-enders trot past; crawled out from his shelter and climbed to his feet.

He coughed, spat. Three riders emerged, ghostlike, from the dust: the Slash S men, riding hard after the herd, and Mack Findlay. Seconds later, his shoulder slick with blood, Eli Simm rode in from the tree-lined ridge.

Findlay drew rein, swung stiffly from the saddle.

'Jesus, Frank,' he said jerkily, 'are you OK?'

'Right as rain.'

157

'It was all I could think of. Stampede the herd, I told myself – and those fellers agreed. And I knew it was a risk, but—'

'Mack, it's OK, really,' Shannon said.

'For you – but not them,' the old lawyer said, and he shuddered as he looked at the bloody mess that was all that remained of the Slash S trio.

'They were dead when they hit the ground,' Shannon said. 'And we thought you were, too,' he said as Eli Simm eased himself painfully from the saddle.

'Hah!' The bony marshal's white eye gleamed in a face caked with dust and sweat. His teeth were bared in a mocking grin. 'What you told me was, if there was trouble, it'd be over in a blink. Well, I heard a shot, blinked – and the next thing I know is I'm hit by a chunk of hot lead and there's a herd stampeding.'

Shannon returned the grin. 'Yeah, but you recovered, played your part – and now I guess it's over.'

'That it is,' Findlay said, 'and everything's real tidy. Those boys will follow the steers until they reach the creek and drink their fill, then move them back to home pasture. And ownership of Slash S naturally reverts to your pa now that his brother's been killed in a tragic accident.'

Shannon took a deep breath.

'My pa's brother was shot dead robbing a bank in Fort Davis.'

'News to me,' Findlay said, and winked at Marshal Eli Simm. 'John Shannon came north to claim his inheritance, brought his own lawyer so it was all legal. He did a fine job of running Slash S and the Aberdeen Angus herd for a year while his brother rested out on Sweetwater Creek, enjoyed life, got his health back. By and by those fine cattle were ready for market, but ten miles into a cattle drive a freak storm caused a stampede and poor old John Shannon. . . .'

Findlay shrugged, waited.

'Yeah,' Frank Shannon said after a few moments. 'Yeah, I guess I wasn't thinking straight. That's exactly the way it happened.'

Solemnly he shook Mack Findlay by the hand, received a nod of reassurance from the wounded Eli Simm. And as the thunder of the stampeding herd faded to a whisper and they began digging shallow graves for the bloody remains of Lancer, Dyson and Bamber, Frank Shannon knew he had achieved what he set out to do. He had discovered the truth.

The fact that it was a sanitized version of that truth that would reach the ears of an old man was something that he could easily learn to live with. Thanks to him, Tom Shannon was coming home.